THIS TIME AROUND
Published by C. KAYE BOOKS
Copyright © 2016 by C. Kaye
978-0-9982167-1-3

Printed in the USA.

Cover Design and Interior Format

This Time
AROUND

OUR TIME FOR LOVE

C. KAYE

"If somebody is gracious enough to give me a second chance, I won't need a third."
—Pete Rose

To my husband who always believes in me.
I wouldn't want to do life without him.

CHAPTER ONE

GEMMA

"SO, WHAT ARE YOU THINKING about the sale?" Tiba asks me yet again.

"Tiba, they are not going to get rid of us. We have a great clientele." *It has to work out. I have Charley to support.* This same thought has gone through my mind since we received the news the regional company that owns our small beauty salon has been sold to a larger international company.

"I just wish that someone would let us know something. I mean, we get word this is happening but then it's total silence. You would think someone would be in contact with all of the shops. Don't you worry just a little?" The more Tiba questions our status, the more worried I become but I can't let her know that. I stop sweeping to give her a reassuring hug.

"I may a little but I can't let it consume me. Charley can sense when I am tense and that isn't good for either of us. Go have some fun tonight and get your mind off work."

Maybe if Tiba goes out for the night with some friends, she will come in tomorrow with a better frame of mind. That would make my life easier.

The front bell rings as the door opens. "That must be Max with Charley." As I round the corner, I see my baby girl looking for me. When she spots me her beautiful smile lights up the room.

"Hey Mommy!" Charley says as she runs to me. I sit on the floor to embrace her enveloping hug. There is nothing in the world better than having her little arms around my neck. I never could have imagined how much I could love someone until this precious angel entered my life four years ago. Max stands above me smiling down at both of us.

"Thanks for taking Charley out today Max. I appreciate it. I wasn't sure what to do when Alexis called and said she was sick." Charley's babysitter is always dependable so when she called, I knew she really must be sick.

Max picks Charley up to give her a hug. "No problem. You know I always love spending time with this little munchkin. I'm just glad I was able to be away from the job site today and could help out." He gives Charley a quick kiss on the cheek and stands her in front of me. "I have to work tomorrow, so I hope you won't have any problems with the sitter."

Max and his father own Greenwood Construction but Max runs the company now. His father retired recently and left Max in charge of the very lucrative construction company.

"I don't have any appointments until tomorrow afternoon so I am hoping Alexis will feel better by then. If not, I will just bring Charley to work with me. I should only be here a few hours and Tiba can help me out." I quickly stand up and give Max a hug.

"Tell Uncle Max goodbye, Char, and thank him for your day today." Charley reaches out and hugs Max around his legs.

"Thanks, Uncle Max! I had fun today," Charley says to him. She lets go of him and I pick her up. She lays her head on my shoulder telling me that she may be tired from her day.

"You are most welcome, Munchkin, and I hope to see you soon. Bye Gemma. Call me if you need anything." Max turns to leave and I follow behind to lock the door. As he walks to his vehicle, I watch him leave and wonder how we have managed to stay close friends.

Charley puts her little hands on the sides of my face, bringing me back from my thoughts. "Did you miss me, Mommy?" Her blue eyes stare into mine as she waits for my answer.

"Yes baby girl, Mommy missed you terribly today. I think we will pick up a pizza on the way home and watch a movie tonight. How does that sound?"

"Oh yes, Mommy! Let's do that! Can we have popcorn too?" Her eyes shine with excitement as she jumps up and down in my arms. I laugh and put her down. Taking her hand in mine we head to the back of the shop.

Half an hour later, we make it to our apartment. I always love coming home. I smile at the pictures of Charley that adorn every wall of our living room. Our little apartment may not be very large or filled with fancy furniture, but it is ours. It is big enough for Charley to have her own bedroom decorated in pink princess from top to bottom.

"Char, let's get you a bath before we watch the movie."

"Mommy! Do I have to?" I do my best to hide my smile at the dramatic tone my daughter gives me.

"Yes, you have to." I grab Charley's pajamas from her room. She is still standing in the hall pouting.

"Come on now. You know big girls don't pout over bath time." That must do the trick. She loses the pouty lip and heads to the bathroom.

Bath time is quick when you have a four year-old ready for her movie. She settles in on the couch with her plate of pizza while I put in a DVD. I get my pizza and snuggle in beside her on the couch.

After pizza, Charley lays her head on my lap and continues to watch her movie. Not much time passes before she falls asleep. I don't move because I really enjoy these times just watching my baby sleeping. In times like this I reflect on my life.

The past several years have been a rollercoaster for me. Being an only child, I was always very close to my parents. Losing them when I was 18 was something I didn't think I would survive. Thanks to Max and his family, I made it through that tragedy and came out stronger on the other side.

Max and I have known each other since we were children. Our parents were close friends so we were always together. We never dated each other but after my parent's accident we wound up married to each other. He thought he was doing the right thing by giving me a family and I needed him and his family. We knew we loved each other as best friends, and honestly I thought we could learn to love each other in a romantic way.

Thinking back to the time Max and I were married makes me wonder why it didn't work for us. Maybe it was because he could never open up to me about anything. He has always kept his emotions to himself. The only emotion Max has ever shown anyone is anger. Not that he is violent or anything, he just can't hold his anger in. Every other emotion is locked up tight.

Regardless, he stood by me through everything. After our divorce he let me stay in the apartment we shared. He was there through my entire pregnancy. He even made sure I had pickles and ice cream when I wanted them. He has been the perfect 'uncle' to Charley. Sometimes I think we should have tried to stay together. If only my heart would listen to my mind. I am just thankful we have remained friends once we realized that love can't be forced.

Looking down at Charley sleeping peacefully, I know that I made the right decision. Life hasn't always been easy for the two of us, but we have made it.

Realizing that I need to get Charley in bed, I ease her into my arms. The walk to her room is short. After getting her into bed, I clean up our mess in the living room and kitchen and get ready for bed myself. As I get into bed, my mind wanders to the situation at work. The stress from the unknown has weighed heavily on me. As usual, sleep is hard to find. When I find myself searching for the sandman, my thoughts always drift to Raef Alvero.

Meeting Raef after Max and I ended our marriage seemed too good to be true. Raef swept me off my feet from the first moment. I still remember our first kiss. His lips on mine is a favorite memory. I close my eyes and can almost feel them. My heart beats faster just thinking about him kissing me.

Raef and I could talk about anything and everything. I remember our laughter over the most mundane topics. We always found the humor in things. I can't help but smile while thinking about some of our silly conversations. He was never one to hide his feelings and I loved that about him. Because Raef always talked about his feelings for me, I truly believed he loved me. Sometimes I still believe he did.

When I found out I was pregnant, I couldn't wait to tell Raef. When he told me he was ending our relationship to concentrate on his career with his family company, I made a spilt second decision to keep the pregnancy to myself. I could see in his eyes that he honestly felt he was doing the right thing. I knew all along his father expected him to take the reins. Raef had worked hard to complete both of his degrees for that purpose. I just thought we would be together when he went to work for the company. I remind myself that my choice was the best for all of us.

As I drift in and out of sleep, I know this will be another night filled with dreams of Raef. I tell myself I don't love him anymore. My dreams tell me I do.

CHAPTER TWO

RAEF

FIVE YEARS AGO, I WALKED away from the best thing in my life because my father told me to. Granted, he kept his part of the deal by making me second in command in our family business. Soon I will be taking over in place of my father. Professionally, I am ahead of the game for someone my age. That success doesn't remove the memories from that fateful day.

I still remember Gemma's face when I told her that we were over. She had come to my apartment to stay the night. She typically stayed with me a few nights a week. I preferred her staying with me. Staying with her was too awkward since she still lived in the apartment with Max. I couldn't help but be jealous of the guy. He was her ex-husband. It was a strange situation, so I just avoided going over there.

The night before Gemma came over, we had talked on the phone. Our calls were normally full of conversation, but this particular night neither of us had much to say. I was dealing with the fact my father had given me an ultimatum. In my mind, I kept thinking that maybe she suspected there was something wrong after our call. Maybe her lack of conversation meant she wouldn't be surprised with my decision. When she came in the apartment with a huge smile, I knew I was wrong. She had no idea. In fact, she seemed almost excited. I felt sick as I tried to find a way to tell her we couldn't be together.

Gemma's smile disappeared as soon as she saw my expression. I remember her quietly asking me what was wrong. She reached to touch my arm but I jerked away from her. The pain in her eyes were like a knife through my heart. I couldn't let her touch me, not knowing what I had to do to her.

"We can't be…I mean I can't be…" My raspy stuttering made me think of my father. Remembering the ruthless negotiation skills that he expected of me, I pulled myself together. "We can't continue together. I am going to concentrate on my career."

That is how I wound up not only breaking the heart of the girl I loved, but breaking my own in the process. Gemma's tear-streaked face still haunts my dreams. Her back walking out my door is a memory that I continue to force myself to forget.

Now I have to break her heart a second time by telling her she has no job. The latest acquisition of our company, Alvero & Alvero, is a chain of hair salons. That is how I find myself in this position. I have to handle the closing of the smaller salons like Gemma Warren's. Since I can't put it off any longer, I get up from my desk and grab my keys. The drive out of the city to the salon takes about an hour so I have plenty of time to think in the car. Part of me hopes Gemma doesn't like working at the salon and won't be upset for it to close. The reasonable part of me knows that this is highly unlikely.

The documents I have reviewed on the salon show Gemma and her coworker, Tiba Ramon, have made the small salon a profitable venture. Even though it turns a profit, the salon is not a good fit for our company

Alvero & Alvero is a top fashion and beauty company with salons and boutiques in large metropolitan areas all over the world. With this acquisition these small shops will be closed and a few of our larger chain shops will be dispersed to the area. Unfortunately, Granier isn't a location that will be on the list for one of our salons.

When I reach the salon, I see that it is in a revitalized downtown area. It's in an older building that looks sleek and modern for the area. It isn't so modern that it detracts from the older feel of the area but it definitely stands out. I am immediately curious about the inside. Parking is a bit of an issue in this part of town. I notice the Mercedes I drive seems a bit out of place with the economy cars and trucks in the area. I realize my suit is also out of place. I don't normally feel self-conscious in situations, but I must admit that I am feeling that way right now.

As I step into the salon, I feel taken back in time and into the future all at the same time. My immediate impression is to be quite impressed with the décor of the building. The original brick walls are exposed with exquisite molding around the ceiling. All of the original architecture is a bold highlight. In stark contrast, the salon furnishings and décor have a modern influence. Someone with obvious talent has had a hand in decorating this place. It's a shame that we are going to have to close this one. Our company likes to make a statement and this place does just that.

"Hi! May I help you in some way?" My attention is brought to the young woman speaking to me while she works on a client. Since this isn't Gemma, I have to assume she is Tiba. I am disappointed when I realize she is the only one here. I let out the nervous breath I have been holding.

"Yes, I believe you can. I am looking for Tiba Ramon and Gemma Warren. I have some business that I need to discuss with them." I'm not sure if she will guess I am from the new owners or think I am a salesman, but I don't want to give too much away just yet.

"Well you have found Tiba; that's me," she responds in her bubbly manner. I don't think she has figured out who I am yet. "If you would like to have a seat, Gemma should be in any time now. Today is her day to come in after lunch." She points to a row of chairs along the front window.

As I sit, I notice not only the normal stacks of hair and beauty magazines that you usually find in salons, but there are also novels on the tables. This place could easily be in the city. Taking in every detail, I decide that we need to replicate this salon in New Orleans. It would fit into our city very well.

The ding of the front door catches my attention and I turn to see Gemma. She doesn't notice me, giving me a moment to enjoy the sight of her. She is just as ravishing as she was five years ago. Her long dark hair flows down her back bringing back memories of my fingers tangled in it as we made love. My breath is taken away. Totally unprepared for the feelings that have come rushing back, I realize I must pull myself together.

"Hey, Tiba!" Gemma calls out. "How has your morning been? Hey, Joann! Good to see you again!" Her voice is still so sweet and hits me right in the heart. I know right at this moment I still love her. That realization shocks me. How had I convinced myself that I was over her? How can I do what I have to do for my company when all I want to do is pull her into my arms and beg her forgiveness? First things first, I have to let her know I am here. Taking a deep breath to calm myself, I stand up as Tiba answers Gemma.

"Hey, Gem. We have this gentleman here to see us." Tiba looks toward me, "Sorry, I didn't even ask your name."

Gemma turns my way. Her smile immediately leaves her face and her expression changes to something I can't interpret. It almost looks like fear.

"I should apologize. I didn't offer my name. I am with Alvero & Alvero, the company that purchased the line of salons that owned this location. I wanted to sit down with the two of you and discuss business if you have some time this afternoon." I turn towards Gemma. She is still just staring at me with that odd expression. I have to make her talk to me. "Gemma, it's good to see you again. How have you been?"

CHAPTER THREE

GEMMA

RAEF ALVERO IS STANDING IN my salon. Raef Alvero is talking to me. What is he saying to me? Think, Gemma, think before you speak.

"Um...hi, Raef." Brilliant, Gemma. That's all I could get out of my mouth. He walks toward me. Tiba carefully watches the odd exchange happening in front of her. She knows nothing about Raef. We have never discussed my past other than the fact that Charley's father left me and doesn't know anything about his daughter. Names were never important before. It looks like they will be now.

"You look great, Gemma," Raef says in a quiet voice. He stands right in front of me now. I can't seem to move and my heartbeat has to be making noise. Can he hear it? Surely he must as hard as it is beating. Why can he still get to me this way?

"Um...thanks." There I go again with the brilliant response. I have to get it together. "So you are telling me that you own our salon? You are my boss?"

"Yes, I guess that is one way to look at it. Our company now owns this salon. The final paperwork was just completed recently. I am now communicating with the salons." Raef still stares at me as he speaks. Tiba continues to look confused by the fact I know this man.

My emotions are all over the place as I walk to my station. Seeing Raef was so unexpected. I never expected to see him again, much less here in my salon. When I reach my station, I notice the multiple pictures of Charley. I stop breathing. Raef's footsteps behind me make me look up to see him in the mirror. I see him staring at the pictures.

Raef's expression changes from curious to recognition. Charley has his intensely blue eyes and his black curly hair. Even though my hair is dark, there has never been any doubt that Charley took after Raef. There is no way to hide that he is her father. He tries to form words, opening and closing his mouth, yet no sound comes out. I can't turn around and look at him. Frozen in place, I watch him in the mirror without any idea of what to do or say.

When Raef finally speaks, it is almost a whisper. "Who is she, Gemma? Who is she?"

My body shakes as I speak. "My daughter, Charlotte." Tiba, in the mirror, gives us both a strange look, still very confused. With a quick shake of my head, I let her know to keep quiet. I will be forced to tell her everything later.

"Charlotte," Raef states. "She is mine isn't she? She looks just like my sister as a child. How could you not tell me I have a child, Gemma? How could you keep that from me?" Raef's voice increases from a whisper into a full, angry voice. His blue eyes, so very blue, flash with anger.

I turn to face him, but can't look him in the eye. "Yes, Raef, she is your daughter."

Those words do nothing to calm him. "I have a daughter! What the fuck Gemma? Why have you kept her from me?" Raef walks in circles as he runs his hands through his hair. I have only seen him angry a few times, but nothing compared to this. Tiba slips into the office area to give us some space. Thank goodness her customer has left the shop.

"I didn't mean to, Raef. I just couldn't find a way to tell you. You had the big job in your family business…I didn't want to ruin that for you by holding you down with a baby." I stutter through my explanation. I never planned on him knowing about Charley.

"I can't even comprehend this. I have a child. Did you know you were pregnant when we split? Why didn't you tell me before we broke up? Or at least call me after? Didn't you think this was something I should know?"

"Raef, I found out the day before you left me. I just couldn't tell you after that. After a while, it just became Charley and me. I am so sorry, Raef. I really don't know how to tell you how sorry I am right now." Tears pour down my face as I finally look up into Raef's eyes. The door opens and my client walks in. I quickly reach for some tissue from my station.

Raef has a hand in his hair and the curls are taking over from the mess he has made of it. "I don't know what to do right now, Gemma. If I stay here this is going to end badly so I am leaving. We are going to discuss this very soon, but I need to calm down first." Raef storms out, slamming the door behind him.

Tiba immediately runs to me, grabbing me into a hug. "Gem, I am so sorry. I had no idea. What can I do?" As I pull back, I give her a half smile.

"Tiba…" I sob into her shoulder, ready to tell her

everything. Pulling back, I shake my head while pressing the tissue to my eyes. "Come over tonight. Please." I hug Tiba once more, take a deep calming breath and head back to my client.

CHAPTER FOUR

RAEF

WHEN I FINALLY REACH MY car, I just sit for a few minutes, thoughts spinning in my head. I feel like I have been punched in the stomach. I have a daughter. How did I not know? How has she been out there all this time without me knowing? Was I so wrapped up in my career that I just ignored something I should have known?

As I sit in my car, my mind fills with anger again. How could Gemma keep my child from me? She has had five years to tell me. Even so, I can't help but wonder if all the blame lies with her. Is this partly my fault for bowing to my father's will? Things would have been so different if I hadn't walked away when he told me to.

Suddenly I realize that I have another emotion running through me—fear. I know nothing about children. What if this little girl doesn't like me? I mean, I will be nothing more than a stranger to her. I don't even begin to know how to build a relationship with my daughter. And what about Gemma? As angry as I am, my feelings for her have still roared to the surface. I don't know how to handle them. After all that has happened, does she have any feelings left for me?

I pull into traffic and head back to New Orleans. I have almost an hour drive to try to clear my head. As I keep replaying the scene in the salon over and over in my mind, I suddenly realize that I didn't even do what I went there to do. My father is going to be all over me for this one. I can't worry about that right now. I have to deal with this other situation first.

The drive passes quickly since I am preoccupied. I walk into my office throwing my keys across my desk. I stand there and look around the finely outfitted office that I call mine. The last four years have been spent in this office. The plan is for my father to slowly back out of the business into retirement and for me to begin to take over in his place. My brother has no interest in the business and my sister is satisfied with her modeling career. This office showcases everything I have spent years working for. No family pictures adorn the desk or bookcase. Only fine art hangs on the wall. Small sculptural pieces fill the bookcase. This is the office of a man with little outside interests. My head spins again wondering where this life fits into the news I just stumbled across.

The office door opens and my father, Charles Raeford Alvero, Sr., walks through it. "How did it go, Son? Any problems delivering the news to the little shop?"

I look up at the man that has always been my idol. I have no idea how to tell him what I just discovered. He will never understand. Leaving Gemma was his idea to begin with.

Love at this age only gets in the way of your future, Son.

Those words have played in my head many times over the past few years when I have missed Gemma.

Dad's way was always best and has gotten me where I am today.

"I didn't tell them, Dad. I will have to revisit this later." I walk around my desk. When I look up at him, I see the disappointment in his eyes. This is the look I have always hated from him. The same look that made me feel unworthy when I was seven and struck out in the ninth inning. The same look that made me feel stupid when I lost the state debate championship my senior year. It made me sick to my stomach then and this time is no different.

"What are you telling me, Raef? We need to get this plan taken care of. I want those small shops closed before I start to back down my hours." The harsh eyes of Charles Alvero stare me down, making me drop my gaze to my desk. I have to think of a story.

"When I saw the shop and the area, I felt we needed to look a little deeper into it before we make a drastic move. The shop is top of the line for a smaller area and they seem to have a substantial business. They may be a profitable venture for the company if we keep them. We didn't do any research other than the basics." As I take a deep breath, I worry that I may have rambled too much and he will see through me. Although I was thinking on the fly with this idea, I do think it is a good idea for the company. My father may be tougher to sell on this.

"So one look and you decide we need more research. We both know how I feel about the smaller markets, Son. We put ourselves at more risk. However, since you seem fairly passionate about this, I will give you one month. There are only five salons in the smaller markets. Do the in-depth research and let me know what you come up with when I get back from our vacation. If I don't think we should keep them after, then you will have to immediately close them. No loose ends, Raef. This acquisition is going to help us move into even larger markets. We need it to be smooth." Dad turns and walks out of my office without a goodbye. I know this means that he doesn't like the idea at all but is letting me have my way this time.

As I fall back into my chair, I let out a deep breath I didn't realize I had been holding. My thoughts go back to Gemma and that day five years ago.

Could I have possibly missed the signs that she was about to tell me she was pregnant? My mind was all over the place that day. I loved Gemmaline Warren and our future had seemed sealed until my father put his fist down. I remember Gemma standing in my apartment when I broke the news to her. She had been so happy when she arrived. Then her smile was gone and nothing remained but pain. Pain in her eyes, in her tears. I wanted to hold her in that moment so badly but couldn't. I couldn't let her see that I felt the same pain. I couldn't shed the tears I wanted to shed. Was I trying so hard to hold myself together that I missed her need to tell me something so important? Should I have stopped her from leaving and made her talk to me?

My future had always been this company. My college major was based on the company. My obtaining a master's degree was based on the company. My hard work since joining the company had all been a means to an end—taking over Alvero & Alvero from my father. When my father gave me the ultimatum that day, I was heartbroken but focused. I looked past the heartbreak of a future without Gemma into the future of the business world. I covered my pain with the excitement I felt for the future I had in the company.

Missing Gemma then became a part of life. I thought of her often, but I also knew that I was nowhere near where I needed to be in the business world to think about a future with anyone. Gemma deserved someone who could give her a future.

Now with the business falling into my hands within the next year, settling down is still several years down the road for me. I have dated on and off but nothing serious. As soon as a woman starts to act like she might be interested in a relationship, I back off.

Love at this age only gets in the way of your future, Son.

My father's words continue to repeat in my head, over and over. Being Charles Raeford Alvero, Jr. comes with responsibility. That responsibility does not include time for a family until much later.

Turning on my computer, I decide to research Gemma. I have always avoided looking for anything on her because it was easier to live my life without knowing what she was doing. Assuming she had moved on and found someone else was what let me accept my life. Now I find myself needing to know if there is someone in her life. Has she married someone else? That thought sends a sharp pain through me. I didn't see a ring on her finger, so I don't think she is married. Just the thought of her even dating another man has me more upset than I ever expected to be.

As I search, I realize that there is not much to find. There are no social media accounts. Just about the only thing I can find is the website for the salon that includes her picture. I stare at the picture of her smiling back at me from the screen. She is so beautiful,

just as she was when we were together. She looks
so happy in the picture, standing there proudly with
Tiba. There is no way I can take that happiness from
her by closing her salon.

I click off the monitor and lean back in my chair.
What do I do now? I have to sit down with Gemma
and figure this out. As angry as I am with her, I am
fully aware that I am still in love with Gemma. I honestly don't know if I can walk away from her again.

I know I can't walk away from the knowledge that I
have a child. My child deserves her father. The question that keeps playing over and over in my mind is
can I be the man she deserves?

CHAPTER FIVE

GEMMA

THE REST OF OUR DAY passes quickly. Tiba and I finish all of our clients and are finally able to clean up the shop and get ready to go home. I know I am biding my time before Tiba will want answers. Telling her about Raef had never been in my plans, even though she is like a sister to me. That part of my life was supposed to stay buried.

"Come on, Gemma. Give me the story." I look up and see Tiba standing with her hands on her hips, waiting.

"Tiba, let's go to my apartment first. I need to get Charley from the sitter. Alexis still wasn't feeling great today so I don't want to leave her there too long. I will cook us something and then we can talk."

Tiba starts getting her stuff together and I know I have bought a little more time. "Okay, Gem, but remember that I get the *whole* story tonight! I'll pick us up a bottle of wine on the way to your place and when Charley goes to bed, you are mine for the night. I get to ask as many questions as I want."

My mouth curves into a small smile for the first time since I saw Raef in the salon. I may have to tell

Tiba everything but I know that no matter what, she will understand and always have my back. She is more than my best friend; she is the sister I never had.

"No problem. I have held all of this in for a long time. I almost think that I am glad to be able to tell you. Now let's get out of here. This has been quite a day!"

An hour later, I have Charley home and Tiba arrives carrying the wine she mentioned earlier. I work on cooking a quick meal of spaghetti while Tiba and Charley play a board game. I watch and listen from the kitchen, enjoying the sounds of my daughter and Tiba squabbling over the game. Needless to say, Charley is winning and Tiba can't figure out how she is being beaten by a four-year old. The entire situation makes me smile even though my insides are in turmoil. Raef has been on my mind since I left the shop. I have no idea how to handle the fact that he will now be a part of Charley's life. When I finish setting the table, our dinner is ready so I call the two game players into the kitchen.

"I beat Auntie T, Mommy. She thinks I was cheating." Charley laughs as she sits at the table.

"She was!" Tiba replies as she attempts to look angry. "She is a sneaky one." Tiba ruffles Charley's hair as she sits down. Charley laughs again and begins to eat. She knows that Tiba is only joking with her.

"Auntie T just doesn't know that you are a Candy Land™ shark. Does she babe? You would think by now she would have figured that out, wouldn't you?" I smile down at my daughter. She will always be the best thing to happen to me. As Tiba and Charley eat, they continue to joke with each other while I quietly push my food around my plate. Tiba notices but doesn't say anything in front of Charley. I am thankful for that.

After about ten minutes, I can't sit still any longer. I get up and start to clean the kitchen while the other two finish up their meal. By the time they are done, I have the kitchen completely clean except for their dishes. Tiba offers to take Charley for her bath while I finish. Of course Charley thinks this is great because Tiba will let her have any bath toy she chooses. I know this will give me a little time to pull myself together before we talk.

When Charley's bath is done, Tiba brings her back dressed for bed. I have had enough time to finish up the cleaning plus get things ready for the next morning. I learned a long time ago that our day runs smoother if I have things ready the night before.

"Charley, would you like to watch TV for a little while before bed? Auntie T and I are going to sit in the kitchen and talk about grown-up stuff." If she thinks it is something important, my daughter will quietly watch TV and let us chat.

"I like grown-up talk too," Charley responds looking up at us with her bottom lip slightly protruding in a pout. I work hard to hide my grin. She should know by now that 'the face' won't work with me.

"Remember what we have talked about? When grown-ups need to talk, little princesses have to be in the other room. We will be right there in the kitchen where you can see us until time for bed. If you need anything, all you have to do is let me know. Now hop up on the couch and I'll put the TV on your favorite channel." The pouty lip is still showing, but she doesn't argue. Instead, she does just as I asked and sits down on the couch, grabbing her stuffed bear and looking at the TV. I am proud of the way my daughter will listen to me without arguing. After I get the channel on for her, I give her a quick kiss and tell her I love her. She is already tuned in to the TV and I get a quick "love you" back from her.

When I get back to the table, Tiba has filled two wine glasses for us and is waiting patiently for me to sit. As I sit, I take a deep breath and then a large sip of wine. A little liquid courage may be needed to get me through this story in one piece.

Tiba seems to know that I am struggling. "Take your time, girlie. If it were easy for you, you would have spilled the beans a long time ago." She covers my hand with hers for a moment. Her words comfort me somewhat so I begin.

"Shortly after Max and I decided to get a divorce, his parents paid for me to go on a cruise with some friends from college. I was attending UNO at the time and had a pretty large circle of friends from there. Before you say anything, I know you think it's odd that the man I was divorcing had parents who would buy me a cruise. Max's family will always be my family. They are the only family I have." Tiba raises her eyebrow again. I push on.

"Anyway, back to the cruise. It was a four-day cruise out of New Orleans. The girls and I had a great time. During those four days, I met Raef. We literally ran into each other in the hall on the ship. The attraction was immediate for both of us. It felt like a shock went through my body when I ran into him. Then when I looked up at his face, I almost melted. He was gorgeous. He seemed to have felt the same thing I felt. We stood there for a full minute just staring at each other. When he finally spoke, his voice just washed over me. I had never felt anything like it before. We wound up spending the remainder of the cruise together as much as possible. My friends were all thrilled that I had met someone."

I take a breath and drink a little more of my wine before I continue. "When we arrived back at the port, we had already planned to see each other very soon. Raef also attended the University of New Orleans, working on his Master's Degree. He lived in an apartment in the city. Even though I only drove into the city three days a week for class, we knew it would be easy for us to spend time together. That time together quickly became almost every day."

Tiba stops me with a question. "So, did Raef know that you were still married to Max?"

"Yes," I quickly respond. "I never kept any of that a secret. Raef knew all of that before we ever got back to New Orleans from the cruise. After a few months, I had him come over to meet Max. I felt like it was just as important for Max to meet Raef as it was for Raef to meet Max. I was juggling an alpha boyfriend and an alpha best friend/roommate. It could get tense at times." I chuckled as I thought of some of the conversations that both of them would try to spring on me.

"After they met, Raef felt better about the situation, even though he still felt Max had feelings for me. I don't know where he got that idea, but I did my best to combat his jealousy. Max saw that Raef was good to me so he didn't push against us. He really didn't say much at all about my relationship with Raef. Raef and I continued to see each other regularly. I stayed over many nights at his apartment. He preferred to have me stay with him instead of us staying at my apartment. It kept things less awkward for both Raef and Max. As time went on, my life seemed perfect. College was good. Raef was wonderful. Our relationship had grown to the point that we were discussing our future. We had a plan…or so I thought. During this time, I'd never met his parents or any of his family. I thought it was odd but since I really didn't have any family other than Max's, I didn't question it."

I stop again because the hard part is coming. The remainder of the wine in my glass is gone, and Tiba quickly fills my glass again. I glance out at Charley and decide I need a break from this conversation. It is a good time to put her to bed.

"I need to put Charley to bed before I go on. She doesn't need to hear any of the rest of this and certainly doesn't need to see me get upset, which will most likely happen soon." As I stand, Tiba jumps to her feet and puts her hand on my shoulder to push me back into my seat.

"Let me put her to bed. You sit here and enjoy your wine in peace for a few minutes. I will send her in here for her goodnight hugs and kisses first." As I look up at Tiba in thanks, I realize how fortunate I am to have a friend like her. She goes to the living room and sends Charley in to see me.

After we share our goodnights with each other, Charley trots off with Tiba in tow. I let my mind wander back to Raef. He had been everything to me back then. I loved him so much. If I let myself admit it, I never stopped loving him. I keep that love pushed deep inside a part of me where I lock things away that hurt. Charley is my everything now and I don't have time to hurt from things I can't have.

Tiba comes back a little bit later with the news that

she had read two short books to Charley, tucked her in tight and she was already dozing. I refill both our glasses and pick up where I left off.

"Eventually I met all of Raef's friends but not his family. One day his mother called saying that they were having a family dinner and inviting some friends over that Friday evening. She wanted him to be there. He normally tried to avoid these gatherings but he decided he would go and take me with him. I wasn't really worried about it since we had been to all type of functions together. Again, I hadn't even questioned why I hadn't met his family. When Friday rolled around, we went to his parents' house. I knew Raef came from more money than I did, but I had no idea just how much more. When we pulled up to his house, I was in shock. His parents didn't live in a regular house; it was a small mansion. While I hadn't been worried before, I suddenly was self-conscious. Raef just gave me a swift kiss and told me not to worry. He loved me and his family would too. I won't go into the long night we had but needless to say that by the time we left, I had the serious feeling his father would never love me nor accept the fact that I was the person chosen by his son. It turned out that Raef was his father's 'golden boy' that would follow in his footsteps no matter what. His father kept pointing that out as the night went on. Raef had told me his plan was to work in the company and eventually take over, so it wasn't a surprise. The surprise was the forceful way his father expressed his opinion on what it would take for Raef to get to that point. It was clear that a serious girlfriend wasn't part of that."

"Were they mean to you that night? Did they treat you badly?" Tiba can't help but ask. She has had to deal with that type of treatment in her past.

"No, they weren't mean to me. They just didn't act like I was anything important to Raef. It was more of a 'you are temporary' type thing. Raef's mother was actually very nice to me. It was his father that seemed to be the problem. After that night, I questioned Raef a few times about it and he would always reassure me that everything was fine. He knew his dad was intense but always seemed to blow it off. We continued to talk about our future and I eventually let my worries pass. We never went back to his parents' house again. After we had been together a little over a year, I had all the symptoms of being pregnant. I didn't tell Raef because I wanted to be certain first. After I took three home tests that all came back positive, I was ready to tell Raef. I was heading to his apartment for the night so I was excited to share the news when I got there."

I stop again and drink the rest of the wine in my glass. This is where it gets tough to speak. I can feel the tears threatening to spill. Tiba sits quietly. I think she can feel the tension coming off of me and knows I need a minute.

"When I got to the apartment, Raef was waiting on me. I could tell something was off from the moment I walked in. He was acting strangely. His eyes looked sad but he was acting like he was excited about something. It was a confusing combination. I was barely in the apartment when he started talking. The short version is that his father had told him that he would be taking over the company much sooner than he had planned but it meant a lot of work over the next few years and didn't leave time for a relationship. He thought he was doing me a favor by letting me go because he wouldn't be able to give me what I deserved while he pursued his career. My heart broke right there. I couldn't even respond. I just left. I never told him about the baby. Looking back, I probably should have told him, but I didn't want him to feel obligated for something he wasn't ready for. At that moment, I didn't think the news would be well received so I kept it to myself."

Tiba holds my hand as the tears roll down my cheeks. I realize that I have cried more today than I have in years. After having Charley, I haven't let myself cry often.

"After what happened today, I take it you never told him." Tiba smiles weakly in my direction. There is no judgement in her eyes, only compassion.

"No. I went back and told Max what happened. He told me not to worry, that he would get me through it and he did. I dropped out of UNO that same week and started beauty school. Max and his parents didn't want me to do that, but I had to have a quick way to support myself and a baby. I couldn't depend on them forever. I kept telling myself I would eventually tell Raef, but as the months passed, it just became easier to think of the baby as just mine."

"Wow. I knew you and Max have always been close but I never realized how close." Tiba seems like she finally understands our relationship a little better. Suddenly there is a knock on the door. Tiba and I look at each other and I quickly confirm with a shrug that I have no idea who it might be. She waves for me to stay seated and answers the door. A few minutes later, she walks back in the kitchen with Max behind her.

"What are you doing here, Max? We didn't have plans that I forgot about, did we?" I immediately worry that I may have forgotten something with the events of the day.

"No plans. I just felt like something was wrong so I stopped by. I know I could have called but you don't always tell me the truth when I call. Why are you crying? Is Charley okay?" All of that comes out of Max's mouth quickly as he frowns at me and my tears. I quickly wipe them away.

"Raef came to the shop today." No further words are necessary.

"WHAT???" he shouts.

"Shhh, big guy. Charley is asleep and she has no idea about any of this." Tiba pulls out a chair and points to it. Max sits but doesn't relax.

"Tell me why he was there. Did he find out about Charley? Is that why he came?"

Tiba answers for me, "His company bought our shop. He was there because of that. That all turned into something else when he saw Charley's pictures."

"He knows, Max. He knows. He left angry but made it clear he would be back to discuss Charley. I really don't know what to expect but I'm scared." Max knows how I feel about the possibility of losing Charley.

Tension radiates off of Max. "Don't you worry about anything. Mom and Dad will call their attorney. We won't let Raef do anything."

I can't help but smile. Max always tries to fix everything. This is one of those things he may not be able to fix. His parents' attorney would be no match for the attorneys that Raef could hire.

"Don't do anything yet. I knew this day might come and Raef does have a right to see his daughter. I just don't have to like it." I frown as I think of having to share her. Then I put on a brave face and stand up.

"It's getting late and I really need to get to bed. Tiba, you know the story now. Thank you for not judging me for keeping Charley to myself. Max, let it go. Don't be angry. I brought this on myself, and I have to figure out how to deal with it by myself." Saying the words, I know that Max won't accept them.

"You don't have to do anything by yourself," he responds as he too stands. "And you didn't bring this on yourself. That worthless bag of—well never mind—but he did this when he left you!"

This is an argument we have had before. Raef gave me the greatest gift ever in Charley. His leaving me hurt me, but I don't hold any anger. Max, on the other hand, has never gotten over what Raef did to me. If it wouldn't have led Raef to Charley, Max would have gone after him a long time ago.

I push both Tiba and Max toward the door. I am exhausted and really just want to take a nice hot bath. Tiba gets the hint and pulls Max to the door.

"You're a great mom. Don't ever forget that. Relax and get some sleep." Tiba gives me a hug and a quick kiss on the cheek. She turns to Max, "Come on, big guy. Girlie here needs some rest."

I can tell Max doesn't want to leave but I don't say anything so he knows that I really don't want him to stay. He hugs me hard and tells me to call him anytime if I need to talk. I just smile because he knows I will if I need to. Tiba drags him out the door and I close it behind them. Leaning against the door, I stand there for a few quiet minutes. Tears threaten to fall again but I am determined not to cry for Raef Alvero any more tonight.

CHAPTER SIX

RAEF

THE NUMBERS ON THE SCREEN do nothing to improve my mood. I have spent the better part of the week doing just what I told my father I would do—going over the records of the smaller salons. No matter how I spin it, the only profitable of the five is the one where Gemma works. It seems both Gemma and Tiba are willing to work hard by doing events such as weddings and it has impacted the bottom line in a very positive way. Unfortunately, I can't justify anything in keeping the other four salons and I feel sure that my father will not consider just keeping the one.

Delving into these records kept my mind busy all week but it has not kept it away from the biggest issue I have ever faced; what to do about my child. Who knew I would be wondering about my future as a father? A week ago, my biggest concerns were all work related. There was never much time for a personal life so there were never personal problems.

There were always women willing to attend events with me when needed. I never really dated anyone for any period of time. If they started acting needy in any way, then they no longer were in my life. I didn't really analyze why, I just attributed it to my hectic work schedule. My feelings were closed off to all of them.

The sudden buzz of my office phone brings my attention back to the present.

"Yes, Ashley, what is it?" I answer tersely.

"I am sorry to bother you, Raef, but there is a Gemma Warren on the line for you. I tried to get her to leave a message, but she is insistent. Do you want me to tell her you are in a conference?"

I stop breathing. I quickly tell Ashley to put the call through, not wanting to risk Gemma hanging up. I feel sure my assistant wonders what is wrong with me. I never sound emotional, yet I feel certain that I just did.

The call rings through and I nervously answer, "Raef Alvero."

"He…Hello, Raef," Gemma's soft voice stutters. My breath hitches just like it always has when she speaks my name.

"Gemma, I didn't expect to hear from you. Is there something you need? Is Charlotte okay?" I realize I sound a little over anxious and mentally berate myself.

"Yes—no—I mean Charley is fine. I just feel like it's time for you to meet her. That is…if you want to. If you don't, I understand. I couldn't handle the stress of waiting to hear from you. I'm rambling so I guess I just need to ask if you want to meet your daughter."

"I do want to meet her, but I'm nervous. That's one of the reasons I haven't contacted you yet. I don't really know what she knows about me. I'm sure she has had to ask at some point, hasn't she? Can you tell me what you've told her?" I'm not really sure I want to hear the answer to that question, but it is something I need to know before I meet Charlotte.

"Yes, she has asked a few times. All I've told her is that her daddy has a very important job and it keeps him too busy to see us. I've never told her anything permanent to rule out knowing you. I'm sorry, Raef." Gemma's voice gets even softer if that is possible. I can hear her quietly crying as she speaks. "I never meant to intentionally keep her from you. It just happened. Please don't hold that against Charley."

Gemma's tears make all of the anger go away. This is the woman that I loved and truth be told, I still love. We have made a child together. I know this moment will define my future relationship with my daughter.

"Don't cry, Gem. I was angry at first but I realize that I am at fault in this situation also. I walked away from you. I would never hold any of this against our child. I do want to meet her as soon as possible. Do you think we could get together this evening or is that too soon?" Suddenly I am anxious to meet my daughter, still nervous but excited.

"Oh, okay. That's quick but I can make it work. I don't want to keep her from you any longer. You've missed enough time with her as it is. I want her to be comfortable so do you mind coming to our apartment? I think it may be easier on her to be in our home where she feels safe." I can tell Gemma is holding her breath waiting for my answer.

"That will be fine. Whatever you think is best. Just tell me what time and your address. I will be there."

I can hear the relief in her voice as Gemma gives me the address of their apartment. We settle on six o'clock and end the call. I suddenly realize tonight might very well be the most important night of my life. Knowing I will not get any work done today, I decide to leave the office and pick up a gift for my daughter. Now I just have to figure out what little girls like. I sure have a lot to learn.

CHAPTER SEVEN

GEMMA

WELL, THAT WAS A BIT of a shock. I guess I should have realized Raef wouldn't want to wait any longer to meet Charley. I just wasn't prepared for him to want to do it today. I quickly call my last two appointments of the day and reschedule them.

"Tiba, I'm leaving. Raef wants to meet Charley tonight. Heading to pick her up." I glance over my shoulder as I grab my things from my station. Tiba's shocked expression mirrors what mine must have looked like a few minutes ago.

"Wow! He doesn't waste any time. Are you ready for this?"

"Truthfully? No." I smile weakly. "But, what choice do I have?"

"You've got this, girlie. Call me if you need me." Tiba gives me a hug before I leave.

The drive to our apartment complex is short. Alexis is surprised to see me so early. We chat a few minutes and then Charley and I are on our way to our apartment. It's just a short walk between the two apartments.

"You picked me up early today, Mommy." Charley

smiles at me. When she sees the stress on my face, her smile drops. "Are you okay?"

"I'm fine, baby girl. I have something I need to tell you. Sort of a surprise." I try to smile in a way to convince her.

"A good surprise, Mommy?"

"Yes. A very good surprise." Charley doesn't seem totally convinced with my answer. "Let's get inside and get you some juice."

I get Charley settled at the kitchen table. She bounces in her seat with excitement but her little face is scrunched like she isn't sure if she is supposed to be excited. I decide I had better just jump in and tell her what is about to happen.

"Do you remember how I told you about your daddy's busy job that keeps him from coming to see you?" Charley nods and stops bouncing. "Well, his job has gotten a lot better and less busy. That means he has time to see you now. In fact, he's coming here today to meet you. Isn't that exciting?" I give my tone of voice a lift on the last part.

"He really wants to meet me?" Charley tilts her head to the side. Her eyes are open much wider than normal.

"Yes, baby girl. He really wants to meet you."

"Oh." She begins to twist her hands, a nervous trait she inherited from me. "I've never had a daddy before. What's it like?" I motion for her to get into my lap. She seems happy to oblige me.

"Having a daddy is great. Remember all of the stories I've told you about my daddy?" Charley nods again.

"But, what if my daddy doesn't like me?" Her big eyes implore me.

"Your daddy is going to love you." I kiss the tip of her nose. "He's very excited to meet you."

Charley wrings her hands again. I tilt her chin so that she will look at me. "What's the matter, Char?"

"My daddy won't try to take me away, will he?" Her voice is so quiet I barely hear her words. She shakes in my lap. I hug her to me tightly.

"No, baby. He won't take you away. He is just going to come here and see you." Who knew that a four-year old would have these thoughts. Her little arms wrap around my neck. Suddenly she sits up straight.

"Mommy, can Uncle Max be here? He will make sure I don't get taken away." Charley nods the entire time she talks. I have no idea where her sudden fear of being taken comes from.

"You aren't going to be taken away, but if you want Uncle Max here then I will ask him to come over." My answer satisfies her. "But, Char, why do you think someone would take you away from here?"

"Bobby got taken away from his mommy." I had completely forgotten that story. Bobby stays with Alexis after school. His mother got mixed up with some things she shouldn't have and Bobby was sent to his grandparents for a few months. He must have talked to Charley about what happened.

"That was something totally different. Bobby's mom couldn't keep him for a little while so he had to go to his grandparents. Nothing like that will happen with you." Charley scrunches her nose like she still doesn't believe me.

"Oh. Well, if Uncle Max is here it will be okay. Can I dress up to meet my daddy?" And just like that, the subject changes. I smile at my now exuberant four-year old.

"Sure you can. Go pick out what you want to wear and let me call Uncle Max." Charley jumps out of my lap without a response and runs to her room.

I make a quick call to Max and as expected, he will be here soon. The next half-hour is spent getting Charley dressed in her favorite dress and fixing her hair just so. She is very particular for a child her age. I can only imagine what she will be like as a teenager. I chuckle to myself. Raef has no idea how headstrong his daughter can be.

I leave Charley to play in her room when I hear a knock on the door. I open it to a scowling Max. I step aside and let him in.

"Are you sure you want to do this? What if he meets Charley and then disappears again? What then?" The questions pour out of Max as he runs his hand through is hair.

"I don't have a choice, Max. Plus, Charley deserves to know her father and Raef deserves the chance to know her. I just have to believe that he'll want to be a part of her life from this point on. If not, I'll cross that bridge when it happens. This is for the best—for Charley and for me." I add the last part in almost a whisper. Max jerks his head up and pins me with those green eyes of his. They are like ice as he responds.

"What does that mean, Gemma? You can't give him a second chance! After he left you!" He turns from me in obvious disgust. Before I have a chance to answer his questions, there is another knock on the door. Raef is here. Max turns quickly back to me. His eyes are on me again but this time filled with questions. I give him a small shake of my head.

Taking a deep breath to prepare myself, I open the

door to Raef shifting from foot to foot. I smile at his nervousness. The sight of him at my door takes my breath away. It is almost unbelievable to me that he is here. Old feelings come roaring back. I have to remember that this visit is not about me, but about my daughter—our daughter.

"Come in Raef. You're a little early."

Raef looks at me anxiously. "I'm sorry. I was just excited and nervous and couldn't wait any longer." I notice he has a package in his hands that he has obviously brought for Charley. I choose not to say anything about it as he steps inside.

I immediately sense the tension coming off of Raef.

"What is he doing here?" Raef questions as he is looks at Max. "I thought it was going to just be us."

"Max, please go get Charley from her room." Max nods but doesn't speak. His jaw twitches. I know he is still as tense as he was when he arrived. I beg him with my eyes to calm down and not cause a problem. He must sense what I am asking since he heads down the hall.

"Charley asked for him to be here. Please don't take offense to that. Max is her safety net. She feels better meeting you with him here." I hope Raef understands.

Raef lets out a breath and nods. "I'm sorry. I just wasn't expecting him. If she wants him here, then he should be here." Suddenly his shoulders tense. "You two aren't together, are you?"

"No. Why would you even think that?" I can't help but wonder where that thought came from.

"I don't know. I just wanted to make sure. I don't know anything about what has happened all this time. I don't know if you have someone in your life or not."

Before I can answer, I hear soft talking and turn back to see Max and my sweet little girl coming toward us. I see Raef out of the corner of my eye as he shifts from foot to foot again, like he can't be still.

"Just be yourself and she will love you," I whisper to Raef without looking his direction.

Max and Charley stop a few steps in front of us. Charley looks up at me then over to Raef. She isn't smiling but she doesn't seem upset. She is still holding Max's hand though, so I know she is feeling slightly timid. I bend down and hold out my arms to give her a quick hug. She steps into my arms, hugs me back and whispers in my ear, "Is that my daddy?"

Standing up and stepping a half step away from Charley, I look at Raef. He is anxious and looks like he could jump right out of his skin. If this wasn't such a serious moment, it would be humorous.

"Charley, this is Raef, your daddy. He's here to meet you." Turning toward Raef, I nod to let him know he can take it from here. He bends down to be on Charley's level.

"Hi. I'm so happy to meet you. I'm sorry it has taken me so long to come see you. You sure are a beautiful young lady."

"Hi," Charley says timidly. "I'm Charlotte Rae Warren and I'm four years old." She holds up four of her little fingers. "Thank you for coming to meet me." I smile at her response because I know it is practiced. I overheard her in her room earlier saying those same words. I look at Raef and see the tears in his eyes as he realizes that she is named after him.

"That is a beautiful name, Charlotte. I love it. I brought you a present. I'm not sure what little girls like, but I thought this might be something you would enjoy." Raef extends the gift towards Charley. She looks at me to make sure she should take it. I smile and nod so she reaches for it.

"Why don't we all sit down so Charley can open her gift?" I ask looking at the two men. Charley anxiously sits on the couch with her gift, already tearing into the paper. I motion to Raef to sit with her on the couch while Max and I take the chairs. By the time Raef is seated, Charley has already unwrapped her gift.

"Oh Mommy! Look, it's an American Girl™ doll! I've always wanted one of these." She quickly lays the doll on the coffee table and jumps over to hug Raef. "Thank you so much!" Raef is startled by the over-zealous little girl but covers it well as he hugs her back. I see tears form in his eyes again as he comes to terms with the fact that he is hugging his daughter.

"You are most welcome, Charlotte. I'm so glad you like it. I have a lot to learn about little girls but I am glad we are having a good start." Raef looks at Charley with eyes so full of love and longing. You can see the hurt of the years he has missed.

"You don't have to call me Charlotte if you don't want to. You can call me Charley like everybody else." Charley turns her little head to the side while scrunching her nose. "What do I call you?" she asks quietly.

Raef looks at me and then back to Charley. He seems uncertain as to how to respond. I give him a quick nod, deferring the answer to his choice.

"You may call me whatever you want. You may call me daddy or if you aren't ready for that, then Raef will be fine. It's all up to you. I don't mind whichever one you choose." Charley looks at him a few seconds longer and nods her head, not making a choice at that moment. She turns back to her doll, still in the container, and hands the package to him.

"Would you open her for me, please?"

"Of course! Let's see what we can do to get this girl out of this box." Raef and Charley smile at each other. She sits back on the couch right beside him as they work to open her new doll. I know that Raef and Charley need a little time alone so I get up and prompt Max to do the same.

"Uncle Max and I are going into the kitchen to get us all something to drink." Charley looks up quickly and smiles.

"That's okay, Mommy. We'll be fine." She places her little hand on Raef's arm and looks back at her doll. Raef looks at me and mouths a quick "Thank you." I smile in response and head to the kitchen.

I make it out of the room before I break down. The intenseness of the day has caught up with me and I can't stop the tears. Max just holds me. He knows that words aren't needed, but comfort is. He has held me like this many times over the years when I cried over Raef. This time, it is a combination of sad tears for time that has been lost and happy tears for my child who now has a father in her life. After a few minutes have passed, the tears subside. I step back from Max as he continues to hold my arms.

"Sorry, Max. I didn't mean to fall apart on you. This is just so much to handle and it all has happened so quickly." Max wipes my tears with a tissue, concern on his face.

"Are you sure this is what you want, Gemma? After the pain he put you through, do you really want him back in your life, much less in Charley's?"

"I don't have a choice. I deprived her of her father for too long." Tears threaten to fall again as I look at Max, feeling all of the guilt of keeping Charley from Raef.

"*You* didn't keep her from him," Max growls. "He did that when he left you. Don't let him make you feel guilty for anything!"

Frustrated, I turn away from Max and begin to get glasses out of the cabinet for everyone's drinks. "I know I shouldn't feel guilty, but I do. He deserves to be with her as much as she deserves to have a father. It is what it is, Max. Just support it please." I laugh half-heartedly as I pull the pitcher of lemonade from the refrigerator.

"I understand. I just don't want to see Charley hurt if he up and leaves again. And I don't want to see you hurt again either. We both know you still have feelings for him."

When I finish pouring the last glass of lemonade, I look up at Max. The concern in his eyes is obvious. All I can do is smile at him.

"Thanks for always being here for us, Max. I don't tell you that often enough. Let's get back in there. I don't think Raef is used to being around children and you know how much Charley can talk." I hand him two of the lemonade glasses and lead the way back to the living room.

CHAPTER EIGHT

RAEF

WHO KNEW THAT OPENING A doll would require so much effort? After several minutes of untwisting things and unsticking other things, we finally get the doll out of the box. Charlotte talked non-stop through the process. She is obviously a little chatterbox.

"Here you go, little one. This doll has been freed from her box and is now yours." I hand the doll over to Charlotte who stares at it with wonder.

"Thank you so much! I've wanted one of these but Mommy always says we can't spend that much money on a doll." Charlotte's words are like a knife in my heart. Gemma has been doing this alone which means that money has to have been tight for her. I remind myself that I have to discuss this issue with her tonight before I leave.

"Well, now you have one, Charlotte. I hope you have fun playing with her." *Can't you come up with anything better than that, Raef?* Obviously, I don't know how to talk to a four-year old.

Charley giggles to me, "It's funny for you to call me Charlotte. Why do you do that?"

"Because Charlotte is a beautiful name for a beautiful little girl. Do you mind if I call you by your name instead of Charley?"

Intense small blue eyes stare at me as if deep thoughts are occurring in her little mind. "I like you calling me that. Nobody else does so it makes it special for you and me." She ducks her head and with a soft voice continues, "If that's okay."

An emotion I am not familiar with grabs me. The same emotion has played with me since I first saw the picture of Charlotte in Gemma's shop. I place a finger under her tiny chin and lift her face back up towards me.

"I think that sounds great, Charlotte. You are very special and it is very much okay." I am rewarded with a huge smile that melts my heart. As I smile in return, we both hear Gemma and Max come into the room. Charlotte jumps up to show her mother the new doll.

Max thrusts a glass in my face. He obviously isn't happy with this situation.

"Thank you Max."

Hmff is all I get in return. Charlotte is still going on and on about the doll to Gemma as everyone sits down.

"Charley, it's beautiful." Gemma tilts her head towards me as she talks. "You need to be sure and thank Raef again for bringing it to you."

Looking at Gemma, another emotion hits me but this one I am very familiar with. This is the way I have always felt when I look at Gemma. Suddenly I feel a little hand on my arm and realize my mind has wandered. I look into the blue eyes of my daughter.

"Thank you for my doll. I told you already but Mommy said I had to tell you again." I smile at the innocence of her words as she shrugs her little shoulders.

"You are most welcome Charlotte and you did thank me earlier. Your mom is just making sure you use good manners." She shrugs her shoulders again and plops down next to me on the couch.

"Do you want to watch a movie with me?" Those big eyes look at me, imploring me to say yes. Before I can answer her, Gemma speaks up.

"Charley, I don't think we need to start a movie. It won't be long before you have to get ready for bed. Why don't you show Raef your room before he has to go?" Well, Gemma just made it obvious that she doesn't want me around much longer.

"Okay." Charlotte says in a sad voice. I try my best to hide my smile over her obvious distaste of hearing the word 'no' on the movie. She looks up at me with a frown. "Do you want to see my room and my stuff?"

"Of course I do. Lead the way." I hold out my hand as I stand. Charlotte places her tiny hand in mine as she gets up. The little hand is lost in my much larger one. It is such an odd feeling for me to hold the hand of my daughter. I see out of the corner of my eye that Gemma is also getting up. She says something to Max but she says it so quietly I can't hear what she said. He remains seated. We cross the short distance in the apartment to Charlotte's bedroom. She basically drags me inside. I smile at her exuberance. I am amazed by the way she can change from frustrated one moment/ to bouncingly excited the next. I step into a tiny room covered in pink.

"See, this is my room. It has all of my stuff in it. That's my bed. That's my toy box. That's my bookcase. I love books. That's my closet." She rattles off things and points to each. I turn, taking it all in. I have to admit that Gemma has done a great job of making such a small place be a room any little girl would love.

"I love your room. Do you like pink?" I say with a grin on my face. I get a look that says "are you crazy" from the little girl that is my child.

"Yes, silly. Can't you tell that?"

"Well, I thought so, but I just figured I would make sure." I laugh quietly. She just smiles at me and continues to point out every little thing in the room. I sneak a quick glance at Gemma to see that she is also smiling.

She just shrugs her shoulder and says, "What can I say? She likes to talk." We both laugh but it doesn't faze Charlotte at all. She is currently at her toy box, pulling out each toy to tell me what it is.

"Charley, let's you and I get your things ready for your bath. Raef can wait in the living room while we get everything ready, then you can tell him goodbye." Gemma turns to me, "That is okay with you, isn't it?" Again, it is obvious she is ready for me to leave. I think she really wants a moment or two alone with Charlotte before I leave. I really want a moment or two alone with Gemma before I leave.

"No problem. I won't leave until you are done. Besides, Gemma, you and I need to talk about a few things before I go." Gemma's lips form a tight line before she nods in agreement.

I return to find Max still in the living room but he is no longer sitting. He now paces. He notices me and immediately comes straight to me.

"The girls wanted a few minutes to get Charlotte's things ready for bed." I figure that I need to make it clear that everything is fine and I am not headed out the door. Max just stares at me.

"I wanted to talk to you anyway. It has taken Gemma years to get over you. Don't start something here you can't stand by. Don't be the kind of dad that shows up a few times and then disappears. Charley's a great kid and I don't want to see her hurt. You hurt either one of them, you answer to me. Understand?"

As Max speaks, he steps closer and closer until he is only a few inches from me. I know I deserve what he says but it doesn't stop the anger from building inside of me.

"If I had known about Charlotte, I would have been here all along. I'm the one who has missed out on four years with my child. I certainly won't walk away from her. As far as anything with Gemma, that's between us. I may have walked away from her before, but sometimes life gives us second chances. Whatever happens now will have nothing to do with you and everything to do with Gemma and Charlotte. Now, why don't you leave and let me discuss my child with her mother. Alone, that is." We stand toe to toe, neither backing down. The tension is thick and I feel sure my expression matches the glare I get from Max. I hear a noise and realize Gemma is back in the room. The question is, how much of that exchange did she hear?

CHAPTER NINE

GEMMA

SECOND CHANCE. DID RAEF JUST say the words *second chance*? I am frozen in place. I knew Raef and Max seemed to be in a very intense conversation when I entered the room, but I didn't realize just how intense until I heard the end of it. Now I don't know what to do. Does Raef mean we may have a second chance with each other?

Suddenly Raef must sense that I am in the room. He turns quickly and appears to feel as awkward as I do. Max sees me and takes a few steps in my direction.

Holding my hand up, I stop Max but don't look him in the eye. "Max, thank you for being here for Charley tonight. We needed you, but it's okay now. Raef and I need to talk about things." When I finally look at Max, I see his jaw twitch as he tries to hold his anger.

"Are you sure, Gem? I don't mind staying."

"I'm sure, Max. Go tell Charley goodbye before you go." I give him as much of a smile as I can muster. I really just feel like I could be sick.

Max doesn't respond as he walks on by to Charley's room. I turn to look at Raef. Neither of us say anything. We just stare at each other. All of the memories come flooding back like little flashes of the past in my mind. I have missed Raef so much over the years. Can I ever trust him again? No, I have to think of Charley. This isn't about me anymore. I break our eye contact as Max comes back in the room.

Max kisses my cheek and whispers in my ear, "Call me if you need me. Don't let him get anything over on you." He squeezes my shoulder, gives Raef one last glare before he lets himself out the door.

It's now just the two of us. I stand in my living room with Raef Alvero. Neither of us seem to know what to say, so we just stand quietly. At the point I can't take it anymore; I break the silence.

"Let's sit, Raef." I point to the couch as I move to sit in one of the chairs. I don't want to be any closer to him than I have to. My brain doesn't seem to work as well the closer I get to him. Raef looks like he wants to say something but instead just moves to sit on the couch.

"Gemma. I don't even know where to begin. I was so mad at you all week but then I come here and all of that anger is gone. Our daughter is perfect. You've done a wonderful job with her. I'm very excited to be a part of her future. I may have missed a lot but I hope you will share with me all of the things I've missed.

"Of course I will! I'm so sorry I kept her from you. I know there is nothing I can do to ever make up for that. I'll get you some pictures of her from when she was born up until now. I'll answer any questions you have about her too." I know there is so much Raef needs to know, but I am a bit overwhelmed with all I need to share with him.

"Thank you. I want to know everything about her. First, her name; you named her after me?" Raef gives me the confused look I have always found so endearing.

"Yes, I named her after you. If she couldn't have your last name, I wanted to give her a part of you. So, she became Charlotte Rae Warren. The best I could do for a girl. I hope that was okay." Raef smiles at me as I finish. Surely that means he isn't angry with me. I nervously wait for his response.

"It's perfect, Gemma. The only thing that would make it any more perfect would be if she were an Alvero. You know I am going to want to make that happen at some point, don't you? She should have my name now." Raef's shoulders tense a little. He seems nervous about asking, but I knew it would be coming so I am not surprised. Raef has always been intensely proud of his family name.

"I know. We just have to do it to where it won't confuse Charley too much. Would you consider leaving Warren in her name too? I think that it would be easier for her since that is what she knows." I don't mention that it would mean a lot to me also. With my parents gone, I am the last Warren. I would like to be able to continue my family name in some manner.

"Charlotte Rae Warren Alvero. I think it has a nice ring to it." Raef smiles a genuine smile that makes my heart beat faster. "Of course I am okay with that, Gemma. I think it would be a great tribute to your parents to have Warren remain a part of our daughter's name. I would never ask you to remove it." Raef moves to kneel beside my chair and gently wipes the tears I didn't realize were falling down my cheeks. This man has always known exactly how to get into my heart and stay there.

"Raef." I whisper as he drops his hand from my face to my hand.

"I've missed you, Gemma. I didn't realize how much until I saw you in your shop. I made huge mistakes with you. I hope we can get to know each other again. My feelings for you have never left, even after all this time. Please tell me there is no other man in your life."

I hold my breath. Raef holds my hand and stares into my eyes like he is trying to see into my soul. My brain can't seem to form words. *This isn't about you Gemma. This is about Charley. Don't make this about you.* I pull my hand away and lower my eyes.

"There is no man in my life. My life is focused on Charley. This is about her, Raef, not about us. We have to keep this about Charley." The words come out of my mouth but they are not the words in my heart. I can't let him see what is in my heart.

Raef stands. I follow, facing him but attempting to hide my emotions. "I agree. Charley comes first. I won't push you, but I won't back off either. I walked away from you once. That won't happen again. Fate has brought you and Charley into my life and I won't let you go. I can be a patient man, Gemma." Raef takes my hand and kisses it. He lets it go and gives me a true Raef Alvero smile. My heart melts a little more.

"Now, I am going to tell Charlotte goodbye." Raef places his phone in my hand. "Put your number in here. I will call every night to talk to Charlotte." With that, he walks to Charley's room. I stand in the middle of my living room in shock, Raef's phone in my hand. He is going to call every night? How am I ever going to do this? Slowly I open Raef's phone and add my number. I can't bring myself to type my name so I use Charley's.

"Did you get your number in there?"

I jump as Raef comes into the room. He chuckles under his breath. I immediately hold his phone out to him. He pulls up his address book and scrolls through it. He frowns when he doesn't see my name and looks up questioningly.

"It's under *Charley*." I can't look at him. He can't see what I'm feeling. I sneak a peek at him and see him shake his head.

"Okay, Gemma. I get it. I'll text you a little later so you will have my number. Don't hesitate to call if anything comes up with Charlotte. I want to be involved." Raef pulls his wallet out of his pocket and opens it. "Shit, I only have $100 with me tonight. Here take this. I will get you more later."

I am stunned and don't know what to say. I don't want his money. Does he think this is about money? I feel my anger rising.

"I don't want your money! I do fine by Charley." I turn away from Raef because I feel the angry tears in my eyes. When Raef speaks it is quiet and almost calming.

"Gem, I know you don't need my money. I can see the great life you have provided for Charlotte. I *want* to help. You have done this by yourself all this time. Let me help take care of my daughter. We will work out the details later but right now just take this. If you don't want to use it to help with your normal expenses, then use it to treat Charley to something she might want. She is mine too, Gem. Let me help."

I want to argue but Raef's voice cracks; this really means a lot to him. I accept the bill without looking at him.

"I will take it for Charley." I don't say anything else because I don't want to argue with Raef. He places one hand on my shoulder and lifts my chin with the other. I have no choice but to look at him. He wipes the tears yet again from my face.

"Thank you. Thank you for letting me help. Thank you for sharing Charley with me." He places a quick kiss on my forehead and turns for the door. My skin burns from the kiss. My heart has completely melted into a puddle on the floor. Raef opens the door but stops before he walks out. He turns back and looks at me with those blue eyes.

"We made a beautiful little girl, didn't we?" He smiles and walks out my door. I sink into the chair and drop my face into my hands. My phone dings across the room with an incoming text message. It's probably Max or Tiba. Both are more than likely wondering if Charley and I are okay. I force myself to get up and get my phone. When I slide it open, I see that I actually have multiple messages from Max and Tiba, but this most recent one is from a number I don't recognize. I open the message and realize it is from Raef.

Raef: This is my number. Put it in your phone.

Me: I will. Charley will be waiting for your call every night. She goes to bed at 7:30 so call before then.

Raef: Sounds good. I look forward to it. BTW, you looked beautiful tonight.

I read that last message three times, but I can't bring myself to respond. I want to accept the compliment and enjoy talking to Raef, but the fear is too great. I can't afford to let him back into my heart and have him walk away again. The phone dings again.

Raef: Your silence tells me not to push. Just know that I will be thinking about you and what this second chance can mean for us. Talk to you tomorrow night.

Me: Don't you need to head home? You aren't driving and texting are you?

Raef: No, I would never do that. I am sitting in your parking lot.

Me: Then you need to go home. No good comes from sitting in parking lots.

After I hit send I realize that my text might sound a little snarky. I hope Raef doesn't take it that way.

Raef: That is true. I am leaving now. Tomorrow night.

I smile, relieved he didn't respond with a comeback to my text. My phone dings again, catching me by surprise.

Raef: Gem, thank you for Charlotte.

I smile at my phone. No matter what happens now, at least Charley will know her father. I get the feeling he is going to be very happy to know her. I quickly shoot off a text to Max and another to Tiba to tell them I am fine but about to put Charley to bed. I let them know that I will talk to them tomorrow in hopes they will leave me alone tonight. I have many things to think about. Some quiet time is just what I need.

CHAPTER TEN

RAEF

ILEAN MY HEAD BACK ON the headrest of my seat. Meeting my daughter tonight has been an emotional overload. I feel things I never have before tonight. I am just beginning to understand how deeply a parent feels for their child. In the last few hours, I fell totally and completely in love with my daughter. She has easily become the best thing to happen to me and I don't even really know her yet. I am overwhelmed.

Realizing that I need someone to talk to about all of this, I make the decision to visit my brother. Daniel has always been my sounding board. He is not the stereotypical older brother. Yes, we argue at times but he is always there for me. There have been times he has seemed almost like a second father to me. Our father has never been one to discuss anything remotely related to feelings or emotions. He is always strictly business.

I make a quick call to Daniel to be sure he is home and head back to the city. Traffic is light because of the time of day but there is still plenty of time to think about all that has happened. I smile to myself as thoughts of Charlotte run through my mind. She is absolutely precious. Gemma has given me such a great gift. That thought brings thoughts of Gemma to mind. She is so strong and has done a fabulous job with Charlotte. My heart aches when I think of all the time I have missed with both of them.

Before I know it, I am at Daniel's house. I can't wait to share the news with him. I don't knock since Daniel is expecting me. I find him at the desk in his living room, working as usual.

"Hey, Bro. Do you ever do anything besides work?" We give each other the usual man hug.

"There is always something to do. Making partner isn't easy. Haven't seen you in a while. What's up with the visit?" Daniel knows a mid-week visit is odd especially since we've both been so busy with work lately.

"I have something to tell you that is going to be a total shock. I need you to know that right now you are the only one I am sharing this with. I want to tell Mom and Dad in person so I don't want this to get out before they return from vacation. And you know I can't tell Marie anything because she can't keep a secret to save her life." We both chuckle. Our sister likes to talk. It hits me that Charlotte may be an awful lot like Marie.

"No problem. You have my curiosity peaked."

"I have a daughter." I throw it out there. The look on Daniel's face is priceless.

"You have a *what*?"

"Remember Gemma? We have daughter together. She is four-years old. Her name is Charlotte and she looks so much like Marie did as a child I almost thought I was looking at her picture. I met her tonight, Daniel, and she is adorable." I pause as my emotions hit me again. Tears fill my eyes. "I am a father, Daniel. I have a daughter."

"Whoa. This is a lot to process, little brother," Daniel says angrily. "You mean to tell me that you have had a child for four years and Gemma never told you? How could she do that to you?"

"It's okay. Now I know. Now we can make up for lost time and hopefully become a family." I take a breath intending to tell Daniel the whole story, but he never gives me the chance to speak further.

"*Become a family! It's okay!* What the hell, Raef?" Daniel yells. "This *woman* has kept your child from you! It's not *okay!*" My normally unflappable brother paces. I need to diffuse this quickly.

"Calm down! There's a lot more to the story. This was my fault too." This stops Daniel in his tracks. I quickly tell him why I left Gemma. When it happened, I had just told him that we split. I never mentioned the reason why.

"Well, that does change things. Still, I don't think you should trust her. She could have contacted you anytime during the last five years and she didn't. You need to be careful." I smile at my big brother.

"Don't worry about me. I am going to get things in order and then I will make Gemma my wife." My smile gets bigger at the thought. "I will not lose her again. We will be a family soon."

"Really, Raef? You are already considering marrying her? You need to slow down and take a step back. This is too fast."

"Look. I know what I am doing. Just trust me. I am going to head home now but I need you to do some legal work for me regarding Charlotte. Can I email you what I want done? I don't trust anyone but you.

And I need this done quickly." I need to make sure he understands my urgency.

"Of course. I'll make it a priority. You know I'll support you in anything, Raef, but seriously, be careful. I don't want to see you hurt." Daniel pulls me into another hug before I get through the door.

"I've got this, Bro. Just get my legal stuff together." Daniel watches as I pull out of his driveway. I know he's concerned. He has never had a serious relationship so he can't understand how I feel about Gemma or Charlotte.

I spend the next several hours tossing and turning in bed. Pictures of Charlotte with her doll and her showing me her toys float through my mind. I am so anxious to talk to her I actually consider calling her in the middle of the night. Luckily I come to my senses before I make the call. Every time I doze, I dream of Gemma. The dreams are short and each ends with a vision of her tear streaked face. Each one awakens me.

When I realize I will not get any rest, I get up and email Daniel with the work I requested. Since Gemma and I already talked about changing Charlotte's name, I want to have the paperwork ready. I also need to get a trust fund set up for Charlotte. Until we can get documents that fully establish paternity, she is not protected if something should happen to me. There is also the issue of support. I have not supported my child for four years and that changes now. I know Gemma doesn't want to take anything from me so I feel the best way to proceed will be to set up regular support payments.

I get to work early and catch up on everything I left hanging yesterday. The day drags on and I find myself watching the clock more than once. All I can do is wait for my phone call to Charlotte tonight. Finally, the time comes and I can place the call. It only rings once before I hear my daughter's voice.

"Hello," Charlotte says anxiously.

"Hi there, Charlotte. How's my girl today?"

Charlotte giggles into the phone and jumps right into a long tale of everything that has happened during her day. I hear about how her babysitter feels better and how much she likes her new doll. She tells me how she didn't want to mess up her doll, so she let it sleep on the table by her bed. I smile while she talks. When she finally takes a breath I comment on various things she mentioned. We talk for a few minutes more before she says that she has to get ready for bed. I hope Gemma will get on the line, but it goes dead after Charlotte and I say goodnight.

The call repeats itself over the next two days. Charlotte amazes me each night with the incredible details in which she tells her stories. She is incredibly bright for her age. The more we talk, the more comfortable the conversations become. At the end of the third call, Charlotte ends with, "Goodnight, Daddy." Hearing her call me 'Daddy' for the first time makes my heart leap. Tears pour down my face when I tell her goodnight. I sit with the phone in my hand for almost an hour before I get my emotions under control.

The following night I ask to speak to Gemma before Charlotte and I end our nightly call.

"Hello," Gemma says tentatively.

"Hey, Gem. I was wondering if I could drive out there tomorrow evening and take you and Charlotte to dinner." I'm so ready to see both of them again.

"Oh, okay…yeah, I guess we can do that." Gemma

stutters through her answer.

"Great! I'll be there at six if that works for you."

"Six will be good."

"Good deal. See you then." I end the call before Gemma can change her mind.

I keep busy with work until my date with my girls. I pick them up right on time, not wanting to miss a single minute with them. When we have to spend the first few minutes moving Charlotte's seat to my car, I make a note to myself to pick up a car seat of my own. The next hour or so is spent at a local hamburger joint. Charlotte carries most of the conversation as usual, but Gemma and I do get a few words in here or there. By the end of the night, we laugh together easily at Charlotte's stories. When I get them home, Gemma doesn't invite me in and I don't pressure her to.

The next few days are spent at work during the day and on the phone with Charlotte and Gemma at night. We have fallen into a pattern where Gemma gets Charlotte to bed after our call and then calls me back. This way we can talk as long as we choose. Gemma tells me stories about Charlotte as a baby. We talk about the milestones of her growth into a vibrant four-year old. We also find ourselves reminiscing about the past. Gemma reminds me about our frequent trips to the zoo. We laugh about the funny stories we would make up about the animals. I remind her about the times we would go to the river to watch the ships come and go. Each memory seems to draw us closer and closer.

During our conversations, Gemma talks frequently about her work. It's obvious how much the salon means to her. The guilt of what I was there to do when we found each other again is overbearing. I realize it's time to let Gemma know what is happening with the salon. After a very lively conversation with Charlotte, Gemma gets on the line. We talk for a few minutes about our day before I decide to turn the conversation.

"Gem, you know how I was at the salon that day to discuss business with you and Tiba. With everything that happened we never did any of that." Gemma remains quiet, so I continue. "I was there—" I pause trying to get the words out. "I was there because my father plans to close the five smallest salons. I…I was there to tell…to tell you we were closing yours." Even though I try to spit it out, I find myself stumbling on my words.

"Oh." Gemma says the one word so softly I barely hear you.

"I need you to know I'm doing everything in my power to keep that from happening, Gem. I'm working on a solution. Please trust me." I groan at my words. I am the last person she trusts. "I know you have no reason to trust me. I promise you I'll work this out." Gemma doesn't respond so I decide to end the call. I tell her goodnight quickly and ask one more time for her trust. At least she does tell me goodnight before she hangs up. I wait for her to call me back like she usually does, but the call never comes. I finally give up on the call and head to bed.

The next morning, I check my phone to see if Gemma called. There are no missed calls so I get ready for work and head to the office. Sitting at my desk, I consider calling her but decide against it. We will talk tonight. I will make certain I explain in more detail what is going on with the salon.

I have Daniel working on the details of a purchase plan that I will present to our Board of Directors next week. My plan is to purchase the five salons. If Alvero & Alvero closes them, they will be a total loss to the company. With my plan, the company will make money from them and I will save Gemma's job. It is a win-win for all parties. Financially it is not a stretch for me.

When my mother's dad passed away, he left his rather large estate to his only three grandchildren. Daniel, Marie and myself all became significantly wealthy overnight. It was not something any of us expected and we still aren't certain why my mother was left out of the estate. She didn't seem shocked when the family attorney read the will. In fact, she was very supportive of us in our newfound wealth. My portion has been invested and left untouched. I do well enough in my position in the company, so I haven't felt the need to touch Gramp's money. Now that I have Charlotte, I want to make certain her future will always be secure. I also want to make sure Gemma's future is secure as well.

Deep in my thoughts, the sound of my phone buzzing startles me. I really am not in the mood to speak to anyone but I click the answer button anyway.

"Yes, Ashley, what is it?"

"Your brother is on the line, Raef. Would you like me to put him through?"

"Yes. Put him through." Maybe he has everything ready for me. That would be wonderful news. The phone buzzes again.

"Hey there, Bro, do you have good news for me?"

"That depends on what you call good news." Daniel always avoids direct answers. It must be the lawyer in him.

"Is everything ready to go? I would like to take the documents regarding Charlotte's trust and support with me tomorrow and I would like to meet with the board next week." I know I have pushed Daniel to get these things done faster than he normally would have for anyone else.

"In that case, I have partial good news. Everything is ready for Charlotte. The name change documents are ready for you when you decide to proceed. The trust fund and support are ready to go. We're ready to make the actual transfer of the money from your account to the trust. I plan to have you do that Monday if that works for you."

This news makes me smile. I can now take copies with me tomorrow to explain everything to Gemma. "That sounds wonderful! Thank you for rushing this for me. Will you email me a copy of everything today so I can show it all to Gem?"

"Sure, my assistant will do that as soon as we get off the phone. As far as the contract for the salon purchase, I am not quite finished with that. I want to make certain we have everything covered so there will never be a question of conflict of interest with the purchase. Are you sure you want to do this Raef? The amount of money you are offering for this is pretty outrageous considering the financial condition of these businesses." Daniel only thinks in good sound business contracts. The proposal I have has nothing to do with business and everything to do with Gemma. What I want to do is a drop in the bucket of Gramp's money but will mean the world to Gemma. At least, I hope it will.

"I am certain Daniel. You know this is for Gemma,

not for me. I walked away from her and our child, even though I didn't know about the baby then. I didn't stop loving her; I just chose myself over her. I won't make that mistake again. I need to do this for her. I want this to be my gift to her when I propose." The more I have thought about Gemma and Charlotte these past few days, the more I know what I want. Even though we have been apart for years, I want Gemma more than ever. I want her to be my wife and us to be a family.

"*Propose!* Are you crazy Raef? Like I told you the other day, you just saw her for the first time in years! Just because you have a child together doesn't mean you have to marry her!" I can hear the frustration in Daniel's voice. "Think about what you are doing here."

"No, Daniel, I am not crazy. I never stopped loving Gemma. I just pushed it back and made my career my sole focus. Where has that gotten me? Yes, I'm doing very well here in the company, but at the end of the day I go home alone. My future is with Gemma. I think I've always known that. Maybe that's why I never dated anyone seriously after her. My heart was always hers. It just took time for my brain to catch up. I really want your support in this, but lack of it won't stop me." My last words are laced with anger. Defending myself is the last thing I want to do right now. I hear Daniel sigh on the other end of the line.

"I told you I will support you, Raef. I always felt you still had feelings for Gemma. I never did understand why the two of you split until you told me recently. I wish you the best of luck with her. It may not be so easy to convince her to jump into marriage with you. A lot of time has passed. You need to remember that. If you really want to spend the rest of your life with her, be patient with her."

"Relationship advice from you, big brother? That's interesting since the longest relationship you've had is two dates." I can't help but chuckle at the thought and obviously Daniel finds it humorous since I hear him laughing too.

"You have me on that one. I just know how you can be. Don't go in with your guns blazing and expect her to fall at your feet." More laughter comes from the other end of the line. "I have to get ready for a meeting. You'll have the documents on Charlotte within the hour. I'll update you on the purchase contract Monday. You may want to mention this plan of yours to Uncle Dex before you go to the board. He will back you on it, making the board more apt to go for this. Oh and Raef, I can't wait to meet Charlotte. We need to plan that soon. Got to run. Duty calls." With that, Daniel ends the call. Typical Daniel style, he is ready to go so click and he's gone.

Shaking my head, I hang up the phone. I quickly send a message to Ashley to make sure to clear my Monday morning schedule. I also shoot off a message to Uncle Dexter to set up a meeting with him Monday morning. He has slowed his involvement with the company in the past few years, but he is still a very important force in Alvero & Alvero. Plus, he is my uncle. His support for my plan will make me more confident in facing the board and my father.

My email dings. I find the documents from Daniel's assistant. Big brother obviously meant it when he said they would be sent quickly. After printing everything, I spend the next hour going through them word by word to make certain Daniel didn't include any wording he thinks would protect me but might hurt Charlotte or Gemma. Everything looks in order so I decide to send a quick text to Gemma. I don't want to wait until tomorrow to see my girls.

Me: Hey beautiful. Hope you are having a great day.

Our conversations the last few nights have been good but not quite what they were before I dropped the news about the salon. We still laugh and talk. I assure her each night that a solution is in the works. She seems to trust me to some extent which is more than I could hope for. My phone dings with a response.

Gemma: It's actually going pretty well. How about yours?

It makes me smile that she responded so quickly.

Me: It just got better. I have some paperwork I want to share with you regarding Charlotte. All good things. I was hoping I could come to your place tonight to let you look over them.

The little dots on the screen that indicate she is responding is the only thing that keeps me from being upset about her slow response. It does worry me that she is writing more than I may want to hear.

Gemma: I guess that will be okay. You are coming in the morning to watch Charley so you could just bring them then. It would save you a trip all the way out here just for me to read some papers.

I smile again. Definitely more words than I wanted, but it isn't a no.

Me: I admit it's a bit of an excuse to see you two. Will bring pizza. Would it be all right if I pick Charlotte up from the sitter? We can find something to do before you get home.

Little dots on the screen move but no message. I hope I didn't push too far by asking to pick up Charlotte. Relief comes over me when the message pops on the screen and the first word I see is 'yes.'

Gemma: Yes, that will be fine. I'll let Alexis know. She lives in our apartment building. #201. She has a key to my apartment. I'll tell her to give it to you. Go ahead and take Charley home after you get her.

That was more than I expected from her. Allowing me into her home without her has to mean something.

Me: Sounds perfect. And Gem, I really can't wait to see you.

No dots appear. I watch the screen and realize she isn't going to respond, so I drop the phone on my desk. With a deep sigh, I realize Gemma is still trying to keep a wall between us. I have chipped away at that wall for the better part of two weeks. Progress has been made but tonight...tonight I hope to take a sledgehammer to it. Tonight I want her to see that I am the man she knew before, a man she can count on. Tonight I plan to get my Gemma back.

CHAPTER ELEVEN

GEMMA

AFTER RE-READING RAEF'S LAST MESSAGE multiple times, I finally lay my phone on my workstation. Fortunately, I don't have a client at the moment and Tiba has stepped out for a bit. Having a few minutes to think without questions is a relief. The nightly conversations with Raef have become very casual and comfortable. Even with the questions about the salon hanging over us, he still makes me comfortable. I find myself trusting him to work things out for the salon. Every night he tells me he has a plan and his brother is working on the legal side of things for him. I believe him.

Raef knowing about Charley is a relief in many ways. I don't feel like I have to hide any longer. Even though I don't want to admit it, I am glad to have him back in my life. We have laughed so much when we talk on the phone that I find myself crying from laughing so hard. He has always made me laugh.

Sitting in my chair, I turn to look at the pictures of Charley on my workstation. She looks so much like Raef, with her dark curly hair and blue eyes. All she talks about now is her daddy. She walks around the apartment holding my phone every night waiting on his call. I smile when I think about the night she first called him *Daddy* on one of their calls. She didn't seem like she had planned it. It just came out naturally. Since then, it is Daddy this and Daddy that.

All of the worry I had when Raef first walked in here and saw the pictures of Charley has faded away. I should have known she would adjust quickly. Charley has always been strong willed. She is a very wise four-year old. You would think she had known Raef all of her life by the way she talks to him. Poor Raef has had a very quick and very detailed lesson on everything Charley loves. She always manages to find something new to tell him every night. He never loses patience with her. I am sure she will talk non-stop when he picks her up today.

Remembering that I am supposed to let Alexis know he is picking Charley up early, I pick up my phone and send a her a quick message. I'm not sure what I was thinking when I offered to let him go on to the apartment without me. It is going to be strange to go home and find him there. Putting my head in my hands, I wonder how I am ever going to keep my feelings for him from taking over.

Hearing Raef's voice every night as we talk has soothed me in ways I had forgotten. Raef always could make me relax just by talking to me. We've had some fun conversations reliving old times together. When he talks to me, it is like I can feel his voice and not just hear it. It brings back memories of his arms around me. All of the "do you remember when", "you are beautiful" and "I miss you" conversations have made it difficult to keep my feelings at bay.

As we near the end of each night's call, his voice gets lower, softer and raspy. "Goodnight, Gemma" from Raef sends chills through me. His voice reminds me of way he would sound after he kissed me. Those memories become my dreams each night and I wake every morning with him first on my mind. Then I remember that he walked away from me, bringing me back to the present and the knowledge that I can't ever let him hurt me like that again. I don't have time for heartbreak.

The bell on the door rings letting me know my next appointment is here. One of my faithful clients enter. The rest of the day passes swiftly. I absolutely love my job. I get to interact with people while making them feel better about themselves. Most of my clients have become close friends.

Now that the day is over, my mind goes back to Raef. I clean the shop quickly from nervous energy so I can get home. What a strange feeling it is to know Raef and Charley will be there when I get home.

As I pull up to my apartment, I can easily see which car must belong to Raef. A Mercedes in my apartment complex definitely stands out. It is a beautiful vehicle. There was a time that I would be drooling over it. Now I look at it and think of all the things that amount of money could be used for. It still amazes me how being a parent changes your outlook on things.

I stare at the Mercedes for longer than intended. The neighbors probably think I have gone crazy. I take a deep breath to calm myself while I get out of my car. As I walk to my front door, I remind myself, this is all about Charley. I pause with my hand on the doorknob and with one last deep breath I open the door.

Before I can step through the threshold, I see Charley running my direction. She grabs my legs in a hug. Raef watches the exchange from a few feet away, as I bend down to hug her back. The smile on his face makes my heart flutter.

"Mommy, come see. My daddy brought you flowers. He brought me some too but yours are bigger. They're so pretty! Come see!" Charley grabs my hand, pulling me toward the kitchen. "You're gonna love them, Mommy! They are sooooo pretty! Isn't my daddy sweet to bring us flowers?"

Sitting in the middle of our dining room table is a beautiful bouquet of flowers. There has to be at least a dozen roses of different colors mixed with lilies, unusual but absolutely gorgeous. I find myself without words, even though I know I should thank Raef.

"My flowers are in my room. My daddy said I could put them in there since they're mine. You need to come see them too." Charley pulls on my hand again.

Raef leans against the wall inside the room. He looks exceptionally handsome tonight with his shirt unbuttoned and no tie. He is dressed simply in black slacks and a white shirt. The look seems to fit him and is so much more casual than the suit he has worn the last few times we saw him. He has his arms crossed and watches me with a smile. Remembering that I have yet to thank him, I know I have to find my voice and not just stand here staring back.

"Charley, wait just a moment and let me thank your daddy for the flowers," I say, still staring at Raef. "Thank you, Raef. The flowers are so pretty but you didn't have to bring me anything."

Raef pushes away from the wall and steps toward me. Never taking his eyes off of mine he responds, "Of course I did. I wanted to do something special for my two favorite girls. Now, go look at Charlotte's flowers before she pulls your arm out of the socket. We have pizza waiting when you are done." He places his hands on my shoulders and leans in to kiss my cheek. His lips send a shock through my skin. I feel the loss immediately when he pulls away. I stand staring at him as he winks at me and tilts his head toward Charley. "Go on. I think our daughter is a little anxious," he says as he chuckles.

Charley and I head to her room to see her flowers. As she pulls me through her door, I see a smaller arrangement sitting on her dresser. It is a princess vase filled with pink daisies and is as beautiful as my arrangement. Raef obviously has good taste in flowers.

"See Mommy! See my flowers! Aren't they pretty?" Charley runs over to them. "They match my room too!"

"They are beautiful, Char. You did tell your daddy thank you, didn't you?"

"Yes, Mommy." My daughter gives me a look to let me know I shouldn't have to ask. "You know I always say thank you!"

"Just checking. It was sweet of your daddy to bring us flowers. Don't you think we need to go see what he is up to in the kitchen?" My heart beats faster just thinking about being in the room with Raef. He certainly makes it difficult to continue to keep my distance from him. Suddenly Charley pulls my hand, this time to get me out of her room.

"Come on, Mommy. Let's go see my daddy!" Her enthusiasm is contagious. I find myself smiling as we wander back into the kitchen. As we enter the room, Raef immediately gives me a smile and a wink before he looks down at Charley.

"Charlotte, I have your pizza ready. Why don't you and your mom sit down and we'll have dinner," Raef says to her as he holds the chair out for her. Charley looks at him like he hung the moon. Tears try to break their way to the surface as I realize all I have kept from him over the years. As if he senses what I am thinking, he looks at me as Charley sits in the chair. He quickly pushes her chair towards the table and walks over to me.

"It really is okay, Gem. I'll catch up," Raef whispers in my ear. With another quick kiss on my cheek, he pulls out another chair. I think he is about to sit when he bows with a flourish. "Sit, m'lady." I can't help but giggle at his silliness as I sit. Charley laughs and he moves to sit across from me. Raef is knocking the bricks out of the wall I have built around my heart, one brick at a time.

CHAPTER TWELVE

RAEF

THIS HAS BEEN ONE OF the best evenings of my life. Things were a little awkward at first but as the evening went on, Gemma relaxed and seemed to let her guard down. After enjoying our pizza while Charlotte jabbered on about anything and everything, we move to the living room. That is where I discover that my daughter is quite the little Candy Land™ shark. We play the game over and over and the little imp wins every time. It isn't like Gemma and I let her win either. Charlotte is just that good.

Before we know it, the time has come to put Charlotte to bed. Gemma helps her get her bath before getting her settled into bed. I read her two bedtime stories in her little pink room before kissing her goodnight and leaving her with Gemma. I feel like the two of them might need a few minutes alone. Charlotte has things she needs to say and Gemma has things she needs to hear.

Walking in the kitchen I see the mess we left earlier. Gemma had wanted to take the time to clean up after dinner, but I convinced her to let it wait. I wash the dishes thinking Claudia, my housekeeper, would probably faint if she could see me at this moment.

The air in the room shifts and I know immediately that Gemma is behind me. Without looking back, I say, "Is Charlotte asleep?"

"Yes, she finally dozed off." Gemma's quiet voice warms me. "You don't have to do that. I can clean up."

"I don't mind. Now you and I can spend some time together." I look over my shoulder. The first look that passes over Gemma's face seems to be one of fear. The look that settles on her face is uncertainty. She shifts back and forth on her feet all the while wringing her hands like she isn't sure what to say or do.

"Um, you don't have to stay. Charley is asleep. I work the wedding tomorrow. Early." Gemma ducks her head and doesn't look me in the eye.

Turning to face her, I dry my hands on the dish towel. She still isn't looking me in the eye so I move closer to her. I lift her chin with my hand so that she has to look at me. As her eyes meet mine, I see the uncertainty again. Who can really blame her considering our past? Her look just fuels me to make certain she has no reason to ever look at me like that in our future.

"Spend some time with me, Gem. Please?" I can't help myself as I pull her into me and wrap my arms around her. Her body feels so good next to mine. *Please don't send me away yet, Gemma. Let me stay. Let me in your heart again.* Gemma's body stiffens at first. Slowly she relaxes and hesitantly puts her arms around me. The breath I didn't realize I had been holding bursts forth with a sigh.

"Okay."

One little word. One little word that holds more

promise than I could have hoped. This has to be a good sign. I kiss her on the top of her head and slowly pull back enough to see her face. She still looks uncertain but now I see a glimpse of hope in her eyes. *Let that mean she still loves me.* My own hope flares.

Before I know what I am doing, I slowly lean in and let my lips barely connect with hers. It is like a lightning strike to my body. I haven't felt anything like this in years, only with Gemma. Knowing better than to push her, I force myself to pull back when all I really want to do is devour her lips.

"Let's go sit," I say, slipping her small hand into mine as we walk towards the living room. Out of the corner of my eye, I catch her touching the fingers of her other hand to her lips. A small smile slips to my lips knowing she seems to have felt the same thing I felt in that kiss. Patience, I tell myself. I have to be patient. I have to make her realize that I am here to stay this time around.

As I sit, I pull her down beside me. She seems to struggle with whether to stay close to me or move further down the couch. I lay my hand on her leg as I look in her eyes and say one word pleadingly, "Stay." She stops moving and stays where she is. I lean over and drop a quick kiss on the end of her nose. Her surprise is obvious. This brings a smile out of me.

"Gem, I know we have a lot of catching up to do. I have enjoyed hearing all about Charlotte growing up and can't wait to hear more. First, though, you need to hear how I feel about you both. I can see uncertainty written all over you. I want to take that away from you. I want you to feel comfortable with me." I pause to let my words sink in. Gemma has erected a barrier where I am concerned. Suddenly my most important goal is to tear down that barrier. She looks at me warily.

"Okay."

There is that one word again.

"Five years ago I made a decision. A decision that hurt us both. A decision I regret." I take a breath before continuing. "When I found out about Charlotte... Please forgive me for that day and the way I reacted to you. I said very hurtful things I shouldn't have said. I was just in shock. I know that isn't a good reason but I hope you will accept my apology." I look at Gemma, hoping she can forgive me.

"There is nothing to forgive, Raef. You reacted the way anyone would have. I am the one that needs to ask your forgiveness for keeping her to myself all these years." Gemma drops her head again to keep from looking at me.

"Gem, look at me. I want to make sure you know my words are true." She lifts her head to again look in my eyes. "I want you to see that I mean everything I say to you, okay?"

Gemma gives me a quick nod of her head. With a quick kiss to her forehead, I continue.

"You have to know and accept that I forgive you for doing what you felt was best for our child. I have spent the last five years drowning myself in work. My entire existence has been work, work, work. Now I realize that work alone does not make for a fulfilled life. Now I see what has been missing over these last five years. Gemma, I can't go back and undo our past, but I can promise our future will be totally different. One thing I know is I am much more mature now and I know what love really is. Gemma, I love you. I love you even more than I loved you five years ago. I know this is all sudden and may seem like it is moving too quickly but I don't want to spend another day of my life without you knowing what you mean to me. I. Love. You."

A tear slips from the corner of my eye. That tear frustrates me as I am not a crying man. Part of being strong in the business world means keeping your emotions in check. Right now my emotions are all over the place as I try so hard to make Gemma realize just how I feel about her. Tears run down Gemma's face as she tries to absorb the words I have just said to her. I take her hands into mine as she stares into my eyes.

Please love me too, Gemma. Seeing you again has breathed life into my dull existence. Please love me back.

"Raef," Gemma whispers. "I'm so scared. I'm scared to feel the things for you that I haven't allowed myself to feel for years. I don't know if I could survive you leaving again."

Gemma's tears fall even harder now. I hate that I have brought so much pain into her life. I can only hope she will allow me to try to remove the hurt with all the love I have to give her. Wrapping my arms around her again, I pull her to me. Her head rests on my chest and my head on her chin. My voice is soft as I speak.

"Let me in, Gemma. Let me love you. We belong together; we always have. This time around we will get it right because I am all in. I love you." I finish almost in a whisper. The fear that Gemma won't be able to allow me into her heart scares me more than anything has ever scared me before. This feeling makes anything I have felt in the business world seem so insignificant.

The silence in the room is almost deafening. There is a small roar in my ears that has to be from fear. We sit like this for a good five minutes or so. It seems like so much longer. During this time, Gemma's tears subside. Her breathing calms against my chest. My heart beats so fast and hard that I know she has to feel it against her cheek. Our future hangs on the response she has yet to give me. The fear is almost more than I can bear but I know I can't rush her to respond. This has to be in her time, not mine.

After what seems like a lifetime, Gemma pulls away from me and looks into my eyes. She seems to be looking for something. My hope is that what she sees is the love I have for her. She nods like she has the answer she is looking for and finally speaks.

"You loved me before and you still left. I'm willing to try again but we have to take this slowly. I have Charley to think about this time and as much as I don't want to be hurt again, I *can't* have her hurt."

Relief washes over me like a warm waterfall. She is willing to try. I feel alive for the first time in five years. How did I not realize I wasn't really 'living' during our time apart?

Gemma's lips draw me to her again. I gently place my lips on hers drawing her into a kiss. After the kiss, leaning my forehead against hers, I look directly into her eyes.

"Thank you, Gemma. Thank you for giving us a chance. I can't promise I will always move slowly because I want to jump in head first but I will try to go at your pace. You have me—all of me. I love you so much. I will never hurt you again and I will never hurt Charlotte. The two of you are my life now. Everything else is secondary."

I can't help myself, I have to kiss her again. Those sweet lips call to my very soul. Moving my lips to hers, I kiss her, letting all of my love flow through my lips to hers. Her hands move to my chest as I deepen the kiss. My tongue skims the edge of her lips urging her to open to me. With a quiet moan, she opens and I get my first full taste of her in five years. I respond with a moan of my own and tangle my hand into her hair, shifting her head to a better angle. Our kiss quickly becomes a passionate mess of lips, tongues and teeth. No one has ever made me feel like Gemma does. Suddenly with this one kiss, I am hard as a rock. As much as I don't want to, I pull back from Gemma.

"Gemma," I say while trying to breathe. "If we don't stop this, I won't be able to go slowly for you." I uncomfortably shift in my seat. Gemma looks down and sees the source of my discomfort. Her cheeks turn a delicious shade of pink.

In an attempt to slow down the situation, I gather the documents I brought with me and look at Gemma. "Let's talk for a little bit about this paperwork so you know what to expect Monday." I give her a genuine smile and run my fingers down her cheek.

"Sure, but is there really much to talk about on a name change?" Gemma tilts her head slightly in a questioning manner.

"No, but I have much more here than that. I do want you to see the name change document just to reassure you Warren is staying. You can decide when you think Charlotte is ready for us to make the change." Gemma smiles as a small tear escapes her eye.

"Thank you, Raef," she whispers to me. Again, I can't resist touching her as I gently wipe the single tear from her cheek.

"In addition to the name change, I have brought documents that will set up a trust fund for Charlotte. This will make certain that if something happens to me, she will have everything she will ever need. You are in the trust documents as the person who will make all withdrawal decisions prior to Charlotte turning twenty-five years old. This will allow you access to the funds for anything you may need for her. Once you sign this document, a transfer of funds into the trust will take place." I hand her the trust document while closely watching her reaction.

Gemma looks uncertain as she begins to read the trust information. Suddenly her eyes become large and she jerks her head toward me. "Raef, this is *so* much money! You don't have to do this! I don't want to be responsible for this much money for Charley!" I can tell that Gemma is getting more upset as she speaks.

"Calm down, Gem. It's really a drop in the bucket of what I have invested." I explain about my inheritance from Gramps and how it is invested. "This is the best way I can think of to make certain Charlotte has a security blanket for her future. I think Gramps would be proud of it." Gemma looks skeptical. "You have no need to worry about the funds themselves. They will be invested but accessible."

"I just don't know Raef. I know you want to do this for Charley but maybe I shouldn't be involved with it at all. Don't you think your father would have a problem with me if something happened to you and I was the one with access to this money?" Gemma seems genuinely concerned about this.

"Gem, it will be fine. This money has no connection to my father. He has no say in it at all. Daniel will explain more to you Monday." I see relief on Gemma's face. Her body seems to relax as she nods and continues to read the documents. I take the advantage and forge on to the next topic.

"Daniel also did a child support document for us. This will provide a monthly amount deposited to your account to support Charlotte." I hand her the papers. Her face scrunches and her cheeks turn red.

"I do not need your money, Raef Alvero! I do fine by myself and I provide for my daughter just fine!"

"I know you don't need it, Gem. But these years that we weren't together meant I did nothing to help support our daughter. That changes now. I want to help take care of our child." I think my voice sounds a little like pleading at this point. Gemma has no idea how much this means to me. I need to know that I am providing for not only Charlotte but for Gemma too.

Gemma no longer glares at me. She doesn't seem as angry but maybe a little torn, struggling with an internal battle on this. I just hope that my side wins out.

"Please, Gem. Do this for me. I won't force you to use it, but at least let me know that you have access to it if you need it. If you won't do it for me or for yourself, then do it for Charlotte." Okay, maybe that wasn't playing fair but I knew that would convince her. Based on her expression I was right.

"Okay. I will do it but don't expect me to use it." She turns her head back to the documents and I can tell she is done with the conversation. I look down to hide my smile.

"Thanks, Gem. It means so much to me to know I am helping provide for Charlotte." Even if she doesn't use the money each month, she will have it if she needs it.

"There is one more thing to discuss, Gem. That's the salon. Daniel has been working on a contract for me that will keep the five shops open. Until I get it passed by the board, I don't want to go into details. The board could still say no to my proposal, but with what I'm offering in the contract, I don't believe they will." The relief is obvious as Gemma's entire body relaxes more than I have seen since I walked in her shop that day. I should have told her this earlier since it obviously has weighed heavily on her.

"Oh Raef. Thank you so much! Tiba and I have been so worried. We didn't know what we would do if we lost our jobs."

Reaching out, I pull Gemma onto my lap and into my arms. Laying her head on my chest, I kiss the top of her head. We sit like that for several minutes before either of us speak. I am the first to break the silence.

"I mean what I said to you, Gemma. I love you and want to take care of you. I know what working means to you and I know how much that shop means to you. You will be there as long as you want to be if I have anything to do with it." As I finish talking, I tip her head upward and claim her lips one more time. Kissing Gemma is quickly becoming an addiction I plan to never give up.

CHAPTER THIRTEEN

GEMMA

RAEF KISSES ME AGAIN WITH such passion that I am almost overwhelmed. His hands roam my body and light a fire everywhere they touch. I hold on to his shoulders as I return his kiss with just as much fervor. I feel one hand slip under my shirt as Raef seeks out my skin. I gasp against his mouth when I feel his fingers lightly touch my bare skin. His kiss swallows the gasp as his tongue easily slips into my mouth, stroking me gently as it does. I meet him stroke for stroke as our kiss quickly becomes wild and out of control.

Suddenly Raef pulls away from me. His lips are still very close to mine but we are no longer touching. We both breath heavily as he speaks.

"Gemma, I can't keep this up and honor my promise to go slowly. I want you so much right now that I don't think I can maintain control while kissing you like that." His voice is barely above a whisper. I can feel his words as well as hear them. I know I am the one who said we had to go slowly but right now I am not sure why I said that. Raef has done nothing but show his love for me tonight. He has given me no reason to doubt him. It's just my old fears that made me say that to him earlier. It isn't what I really want. I want Raef as much as he seems to want me. The war within me to go slowly is lost.

"I want you too, Raef. I know I said we had to move slowly but I am willing to give us the chance you have asked for." I pull back a little farther so I can look into Raef's eyes. They are dark blue with desire and hope. I lean in and gently kiss his lips before pulling back again. "I love you, Raef Alvero, and I want you to make love to me tonight."

Raef's nostrils flare and his eyes get even darker blue. He grabs the back of my head and kisses me with everything he has. I only thought the previous kisses were passionate. This one has us both laid bare. We kiss each other not only with our bodies, but also with our emotions.

Suddenly I am lifted as Raef stands with me in his arms. He barely breaks away from my mouth and says, "Bedroom?" I quickly point toward the end of the hall. His lips return to mine as he carries me to the bedroom. He flips on the light switch and lays me on the bed. He stands and doesn't move but just looks at me. I suddenly become self-conscious.

"What is it?" I ask as he continues to look at me.

"You are so beautiful. I honestly can't believe I am here with you. I had no idea how much I've missed you."

I smile, letting his words wash over me. Then I realize the door is still open. "Raef, you might want to close the door. I don't think we want Charley walking into the hall and seeing us."

"Oh my goodness! Right!" Raef rushes back to the door to close it. "I'm not used to having kids around. I better learn to adjust quickly!" He laughs and comes back to the bed, gently sitting on the edge.

Raef reaches for the edge of my shirt, lifting it. I raise enough for him to pull it over my head. His hands roam my skin as he leans to kiss my neck. He places gentle kisses from my neck down to my breasts. His hands come up to pull my bra downward, pushing my breasts above it. Raef anxiously moves to take one of my nipples in his mouth. I gasp at the sensations that course through my body. Raef moves to the other side and follows suit on the other nipple. He bites down slightly and is rewarded with a moan as I grip handfuls of the bed covers.

I feel the smile on Raef's face as he continues to move back and forth between my breasts. He has no idea that I haven't been with anyone since we were together so he has no reason to know how close this brings me to the edge. His mouth moves below my breasts and he starts his trail of kisses all down my stomach. Those kisses drive me crazy and I can't stop squirming.

"So responsive," Raef says. "You always were so responsive. I'm so glad that hasn't changed."

Suddenly Raef moves away from me and stands at the edge of the bed, holding out his hand to me. "Let's get the rest of these clothes off of you. I want to see all of you." As I stand, he eagerly removes my bra and unzips my pants. I toe off my shoes as Raef slides off my pants and socks. I am left in nothing but my panties but he makes quick work of removing them also.

Standing naked in front of Raef, I move to cover myself. I feel very self-conscious being the only one with no clothes on. He grabs my hands and pulls my arms away from my body.

"Don't hide yourself from me. I love seeing all of you." Raef's hands cover my stomach as he looks down in wonder. "My child grew in you. I missed seeing you rounded, carrying my growing baby inside you. I promise you I will be there for every minute of the next one. I'll watch every little change in your body when we have our next baby." He looks at me eyes so full of emotion that I feel a tear escape. I never expected to hear those words from him. I never imagined Raef and I would have another child together.

My lips turn up in a smile thinking of more babies with Raef. He pulls me into his arms and kisses me so softly I almost miss it.

"I want a big family with you. I love you so much."

"I love the sound of that, Raef. Right now, though, I think you have on way too many clothes." I unbutton his shirt. He quickly jumps in to help and, in what seems like a few seconds, he is divested of his clothing and has a condom in his hand. Not sure where he was hiding it, but I am thankful that he has it handy.

Raef eases me back down on the bed while kissing me roughly. I give back to the kiss with everything I have. We are a jumbled mess of lips as our passion ignites. Raef pulls back suddenly and looks at me while panting.

"I wanted to take this slowly with it being the first time we were back together, but Gem, I don't think I can. I want you so much right now. I promise to treat you like a princess next time, but I can't wait any longer. I need to be inside of you now." He opens the condom and rolls it on swiftly, then moves between my knees. As he places himself at my entrance, he begins to ease inside me.

His eyes never leave mine as I hold my breath while he enters me. He is so large and I have not been with anyone in so long, that he has to slowly work his way in. Enter, retreat, enter, retreat. The pattern of his motions is a little painful but the pleasure is overwhelming. Suddenly he pushes the remainder of the way in and I gasp with the breath I had been holding. He stills and touches the side of my face, his eyes still never leaving mine.

"So damn tight, Gem. You feel just like you felt before. So damn good." Raef begins to move inside me and quickly picks up the pace. I feel myself rising so rapidly that I am almost unprepared for the feeling. Before I expect it, I crash over the edge and break into a million pieces. My moans are louder than I imagined they could be and Raef seems feed off of them. He pounds into me. Suddenly he growls loudly and stills as he reaches his peak. He kisses me with the most tender kiss I have ever experienced.

"I could stay like this forever. But I need to get rid of this condom." He eases his way out of me. The movement causes me to moan again. "Damn, Gemma, keep that up and I will be hard again in no time." He quickly disposes of the condom and crawls back in bed with me. He lies on his back and pulls me into his arms with my head on his chest.

"Wow, Gemma. That was amazing. I'm sorry it went so fast. I plan on worshipping that body of yours in many ways tonight and it will go slower then. Being with you felt just like it did before. I have never forgotten that feeling. There were many nights I dreamed of being deep inside of you. I just never imagined I would have the chance again." Raef's hand gently rubs my back as he talks.

"I haven't been with anyone since you," I whisper to him. I'm not sure why I just told him that. It just seemed like he should know. Raef moans and rolls me over to where he is once again on top of me.

"You have no idea how much that means to me. I wish I could say the same to you, but unfortunately I can't. What I can tell you is that none of the others meant anything to me. Whether I wanted to admit it at the time or not, my heart always belonged to you. I can also tell you that from this point on, there will be no other but you. I. Am. Yours." Raef kisses me deeply. I can tell this is going to be a night where neither of us get much sleep. With the way he makes me feel, I wouldn't have it any other way.

CHAPTER FOURTEEN

RAEF

THE LAST WEEK HAS BEEN wonderful. Gemma and I handled all of the paperwork with Daniel on Monday. Once Daniel explained how a trust works, she felt much better about it. She even decided to go ahead with the name change. She felt it would be better to have Charlotte adjust to the new name before starting school soon.

Every night has been spent with Gemma and Charlotte. Driving into the city every day hasn't been as bad as I thought it would be. That could be because it is worth it. Charlotte has really taken to having a family that includes a dad. She hasn't even questioned the fact that I stay over every night. I think she just assumes that when you have a daddy, he lives with you.

Gemma and I have grown closer than we have ever been. I honestly don't know how I have lived without her all these years. Now that we have found each other again, I know I can never go back to living just for work. My future is fully entrenched with Gemma and Charlotte. I can't wait to make Gemma my wife, but I have not broached the subject with her. She has agreed to give her heart to me, but I feel she is still a little uncertain of our future. I have a plan to make those fears disappear forever.

My plan to save Gemma's salon is about to come to fruition. We have a board meeting to address the purchase in a few minutes. I had planned to wait until my father was home before taking my proposal to the board but since my parents extended their trip I couldn't wait any longer. Uncle Dex encouraged me to go ahead and have it all settled since one more vote shouldn't change the outcome.

Entering the board room, I greet each of the board members. Most have been on the board of Alvero & Alvero since I was a child. After a bit of chit-chat, we get down to business.

I quickly present my proposal to purchase the shops, outlining the amount I am offering for them. Judging by their expressions, they seem shocked with the dollar figure.

"Raef, why would you offer this much for salons you yourself say aren't making money?" John Williams questions me.

"I admit I want these salons for a personal reason. Since our company would not gain anything by closing them without a sale, I decided to pursue them. My offer should convince you that offering them on the open market will not gain a higher price."

"That is an awful lot of money, son. What does your father have to say about this?" I should have expected Jackson West to question me about my father.

"Actually, my father knows nothing about this. He and my mother are on an extended vacation and the last thing I want to do is disturb them with business. As you all know, he is beginning to lessen his workload in preparation for retirement. This is a win-win for myself and the company so I saw no need to interrupt their trip." I speak with a firm voice, the voice I learned from my father.

"It would be bad business to turn this offer down," Uncle Dex speaks up. "Raef is a grown man. If he wants to make an offer of this size, it's his choice. The company will only benefit from his purchase."

After reassuring them that I want this to be a win-win situation for the company and myself, they accept the proposal. We sign the papers and I immediately have Ashley take them to Daniel to be filed. Back in my office, I relax behind my desk.

Pulling the small box out of my pocket, I open it and gaze at the beautiful ring I purchased this week. When I saw it, I knew it was the one for Gemma. It's not too large because I know she wouldn't like something she would feel was gaudy. It has an almost Victorian look to it and just screamed 'Gemma' to me. I have carried it in my pocket since I bought it but was waiting until I could have her wedding gift ready. My plan is to present her with ownership of her salon and the other four my father planned to close.

Everything is ready for me to propose. I wanted to come up with a special time and place but am too anxious to plan something like that. Just having Charlotte with us in what has become our little home at the apartment will have to do. Tonight is the night. Tonight I will propose to the love of my life. I hope she is ready to take that step with me. For a man who can face anything in the business world, I have to admit I am very nervous about this. What if she says no? My mind keeps asking that question but

I just keep convincing myself she will say yes. I can't imagine the alternative. Being so deep in thought, I don't hear my office door open.

"What the hell is that!" My dad's voice booms through my office. I jump in surprise not only because I thought I was alone but also because he was not supposed to be home for another week. Quickly closing the ring box and placing it back in my pocket, I stand and round my desk.

"Well, Dad, it's an engagement ring. A lot has happened since you and Mom have been on your trip. There are so many things I want to tell the two of you but would rather tell you both together. Is Mom at home? Maybe we could head over to the house and let me catch you up." I extend my hand to my father expecting him to reciprocate. A formal greeting is all you get from Charles Alvero. When he doesn't move to shake my hand, I drop mine.

"You don't have to catch me up on anything. I know everything that's happened here and I can tell you that your mother isn't going to know of any of this! You have nothing to tell her because you're going to forget everything that's happened since we've been on vacation," Dad's voice booms again and is full of what can only be described as anger mixed with disgust. I am taken aback with his reaction.

"What do you mean, Dad? There's nothing to forget. I found out that I have a daughter, and I am going to marry Gemma. Why are you so angry?"

"YOU WILL NOT MARRY THAT TRAMP!" Dad screams at me. His face is a deep shade of red. "You don't even know if that bastard child is yours! You are not giving up the life I've made for you for some tramp and her kid! Plus, you are not using your money from your grandfather to buy some lowly little salons just to make her stay with you! I already have the company attorneys working on a way to get you out of that purchase!"

The shock on my face must be something to see. I've never seen my father act like this before and I can't believe the things he just said about Gemma and Charlotte. For a few moments I just stare at him with my mouth agape. The longer I stare, the angrier I become. I'm quite sure my face has turned the exact shade of red as his with the realization of the words he just called my daughter and my love.

"Don't you dare say those things about Gemma or Charlotte! You have no idea what you are talking about. One look at Charlotte tells me she is mine. If you know about her then you should know that. She is an exact replica of Marie at that age. And don't ever call Gemma a tramp again! She is the most genuine person I have ever known. Plus, she is the woman I love. They are my family and I will not have you speak of them that way!"

Suddenly my father barks out a disgusting laugh. Again, I am shocked by his response. "I am your family and I have created all of this for you!" He moves around the room and waves his hands as he speaks. "You will not marry a girl who comes from nothing. Everything has been set for your future here. Hell, Son, I even put Ashley right here at your disposal so you two could eventually marry. Why do you think she works as your assistant? With her family, she could work anywhere she chooses. She is here to become your wife, not just be your little assistant!"

I jerk in response to his last words. Admittedly, I have wondered why Ashley was settling for an assistant position. I had just assumed she really didn't want to have a career that required a considerable amount of time and pressure. She has always seemed happy in her job. Never in my wildest imagination did I think that my father would have placed her here for me to choose her to marry. What could he have been thinking? It seems to me he has done a lot of 'thinking' where I'm concerned and none of it makes me very happy.

"I will never marry Ashley. I am marrying Gemma. She's the only woman I have ever loved. You can give up on any other ideas for me." I speak very clearly to make sure my father has no room to misunderstand my words.

"You may think you are marrying that girl but when I am done, she won't be there for you to marry. I kept you away from her once before and I will do it again. Once you realize being with her is off the table, we will have a DNA test done on the kid. If she is yours, you can pay child support and move on with your life. Your place is here in this company. That requires you to marry well. Marrying Gemmaline Warren is not marrying well." Dad finishes his tirade with another sick chuckle. "Trust me, you won't be marrying her."

"What have you done? And what do you mean you kept me from her before?" Worry flashes into my mind as I try to think of scenarios that involve my father and Gemma.

Dad laughs again. "Oh, Son, you have no idea, do you? Why do you think I insisted you leave her so that you could pursue your career here? It had nothing to do with you not needing any attachments at the time. It was simply who that attachment happened to be.

I thought when I got you away from her, I wouldn't have to deal with her again. Then I get word she has a kid. Of course, who knows who all she has been with so I didn't worry about the kid being yours. Then I have to hear all the way in Italy that you are claiming the kid and are back with that girl. Desperate times call for desperate measures, Son. Once she finds out you have closed her precious little salon, there is no way she will marry you. Problem solved and you can go back to your life."

Fear flows through me at lightning speed. Surely he can't mean what he's saying. I bought the salons so there is no way Gemma would think I was closing hers. Unless my father has done something that I don't know about. The fear of that is so strong I can't breathe.

"What have you done, *Father*?" I say the last word with total irreverence in my voice.

"Just taken care of things for you. As we speak, little Gemmaline Warren is being told her salon is being closed immediately and she is to vacate the premises. It's over, Son. She won't want you now. Give up and realize your place is here, with someone like Ashley. If you don't start acting like the man I expect you to be then I may just have to consider if you will continue to work here in preparation to take my place."

My stomach rolls as I think of how Gemma must feel right now. Everything is being pulled out from under her and she thinks it is my fault. How could my own father do this? His vague threat is meant to make me fearful of losing my place in the family company. All it does is make me realize what I have to do. I can lose everything else, but I cannot lose Gemma and Charlotte. I grab my jacket as I walk towards the door.

"You don't have to worry about letting me continue here. My life is with Gemma and Charlotte now." Without looking back, I open the door just as I say, "I. Quit." Practically running down the hall, I head toward the parking garage. I pull out my phone and dial Gemma but it goes straight to voicemail. My steps pick up speed. I know I have to get to her quickly. She isn't going to answer my calls; I will have to see her in person. The question is, how quickly can I make the drive?

CHAPTER FIFTEEN

GEMMA

IT HAS BEEN A LONG day of work. Tiba and I had more clients than normal today. We don't usually open on Monday, but lately we have opened Monday through Friday in an effort to show that our salon should remain open. Raef keeps telling me not to worry, but I can't help it. He assures me everything is going to be fine and the shop will be open with no changes for myself or Tiba. I want to believe him, but Tiba and I feel the extra work can't hurt.

Things have been great with Raef. He has all but moved into the apartment. Charley loves her dad being there every night. I hate for him to have to make that long drive every morning and evening but he insists he doesn't mind. I have to admit that I really like having him with us. The fear of him leaving again remains but each day it dissipates a little more. It's amazing how we have grown so close in such a very short time. It almost seems like we were never apart.

The bell on the door dings as someone enters the shop. It's late in the afternoon and neither Tiba nor I are expecting any more customers. It must be another walk-in. Even though I am ready to get home to

Charley and Raef, I take a deep breath and turn to
welcome the person. One more customer can't keep
me here that much longer. When I see the gentleman
in the suit I sigh in relief. A quick man's haircut won't
take long at all. I put on a smile as I welcome him.

"Good afternoon! Welcome to our salon. Are you
here for a haircut today?"

"No. I am not here for a haircut. I am here to deliver
a message to Gemmaline Warren and Tiba Ramone."
The young man speaks in a very monotone voice like
he is bored.

"I am Gemma and that's Tiba," I say as I point to
Tiba. I can't imagine what message this man could
have for us.

"Well then, Ms. Warren and Ms. Ramone, Mr.
Alvero has asked that I tell you that this salon is closed
permanently as of today. You are asked to vacate the
premises immediately. Please take any personal items
with you as access after you leave will be denied."

Tiba and I both gasp. How could this happen? Why
didn't Raef come tell us in person? This can't be happening. I can't speak but I hear Tiba speaking to the
man.

"Mr. Alvero sent you? Which Mr. Alvero? Was it
Raef or his father?"

Mr. Monotone looks as if he is exasperated by having to answer Tiba's questions. "I have no idea. I was
just told to give you the message from Mr. Alvero.
Considering that Mr. Alvero, Sr. is out of the country,
I would think it would be from Mr. Alvero, Jr.—not
that it really matters. You ladies need to collect your
things. I will wait outside to lock up and take the
keys." He turns and leaves the shop as quickly as he
entered.

The tears flow as I fall to my knees. Tiba runs to me and puts her arms around me as we both sink to the floor. She is crying too, but I am crying for so much more than just a job. How could Raef do this to us? I really thought he loved me. How could he do this to Charley? My only thought is that he has decided he doesn't want to be a father after all. What better way to show me than to close the shop?

"You know this isn't Raef. This has to be his father or someone else." Tiba holds me as I cry harder.

"You heard the man, Tiba. Raef's father is still out of the country! Why would he send a message to close this place when he isn't even here! It has to be Raef. He has decided he doesn't want me or Charley. It's the only answer." I sob as my heart breaks. I survived him leaving me once, but I don't know if I can survive it again. Why did I ever trust him?

"Think about it, Gemma. This doesn't sound like Raef at all. That man loves you more than anything in the world except maybe Charley. He's shown that to everyone in the last week. Anyone around the two of you can see it. This is a mistake or something." Tiba tries to calm me but it doesn't work.

"It's no mistake. That man out there is going to take our keys. It is over. Our jobs are gone. Raef is gone. It's over." My sobs subside a little as I pull away from Tiba. "We have to get our stuff together. I don't want him to come back in here and kick us out before we can get our things."

We both get up from the floor and begin to gather our personally owned items. Tiba finds boxes in the office and we pack up everything we have. We don't talk as we work. I know Tiba wants to convince me this isn't the work of Raef but she keeps quiet. I am sure she feels the tension coming from me. I don't want to hear anything from her right now. I just want to collect my things and get to my daughter. I have to figure out where we go from here.

Once everything is packed, I look around the room. I have loved every minute that was spent in this place. Missing it is going to be tough. Tiba and I have made a lot of friends through this place. Now we have to call them and tell them we are closed. Hopefully once we both settle into new jobs some of them will come back to us. It will just depend on how long we are out of work. People have to move on when their salon shuts down. The tears on my face are just a small indication of the heart-wrenching pain I feel.

Picking up my box, I look at Tiba. She carries a box also. We both move to the door with tears running down our face. Leaving this place is just as hard on her as it is me. I can't let my personal broken heart cloud that. Tiba loves this place as much as I do.

"I'm so sorry, Tiba. I really thought he would come through for us." Tiba pushes on the door to let us both out. I stop and we both look back inside one last time. Sighing, I turn around and see Mr. Monotone getting out of his fancy car. Tiba and I step away and let the door close.

"Don't apologize, Gemma. This isn't your fault. And it isn't Raef's fault either. I'm telling you, this isn't him. Something else is going on here. Please wait and hear Raef's side of the story before you do something you will regret."

I shake my head. She is trying to make me feel better but she might as well give up. It is over. I have to face that. I give her a weak smile and head to my car. The poor old thing doesn't look like much, but right now I am thankful I don't have a car note. That is one less thing I will have to worry about since I don't have a job.

I expect Tiba to follow me and continue to try to convince me to talk to Raef. Surprisingly she doesn't. I load my things into my car and look back at the salon one last time. Mr. Monotone comes out of the door just as I look back. He quickly locks the door and moves toward his vehicle. The tears flow again as I stare at the place that has been my means of supporting my daughter. Fear creeps in on me as quickly as the sadness has. Sighing, I turn away and get in my vehicle. Staring at the building won't change anything.

The drive to my apartment goes quickly. My tears have dried which is a good thing. I have to get control of my emotions before I get Charley from the babysitter. She won't understand why I am so upset and that will just make her upset. It will be bad enough when she finds out her daddy won't be coming over anymore. I don't need her worrying about me on top of that.

As I pull into the parking lot of my apartment complex, I see Max's truck. He is leaning against the side of it. I pull my car into an open parking space next to him. I have no idea what he is doing here today but seeing a friendly face is a welcome sight. Max opens the door and offers me his hand to help me out of the car.

"What are you doing here Max?" I ask.

"Tiba called and told me what happened. I was in town so I came straight here. She was worried about you." Max pulls me into a tight hug. "It's going to be okay, Gemma. It must be some kind of mistake or something. We'll get it all straight tomorrow."

I quickly shake my head and pull away from Max. "There's nothing to get straight. Raef did this. He took my job away. Tomorrow I have to find a new one." I turn back to the car to get out my box of things from work. Max quickly jumps in front of me and picks up the box. We both head toward the apartment.

"Do you want to run and get Charley while I take this box in?" Max asks as we get to the door.

"No. I am going to wait a few more minutes until I can make sure I have my emotions in check. I don't want her to see me so upset." We enter the apartment door and the feeling of Raef overwhelms me. Everywhere I look in my home, I see Raef. His presence here has been so strong for the last week. Memories are everywhere now. The tears fall again. Max realizes the door is still open and I haven't fully entered the apartment. He gently takes my arm and leads me into the room while closing the door. The tears stream as I cover my mouth with a sob.

"How can I stay here now? How can we be here without him?" I fall against Max as he puts his arms around me in comfort. I can feel the stress in him as I cry against his chest.

"Why don't you just wait and talk to Raef? I can take Charley out to Mom's house for the night. Mom would love to see her since you guys missed Sunday dinner this week. Then you and Raef could have some time alone to discuss everything." Max is acting just like Tiba and I don't understand why. Why is everyone wanting me to talk to Raef after what he has done? Anger begins to replace the sadness. I am angry with Raef. Now I am also angry with Tiba and

Max. They just don't understand.

"I am not talking to Raef. Will you just drop it!" I say angrily as I pull away from Max. Turning away from him, I continue, "I can't talk to him after what he has done! I can't stay here either! He is everywhere I look! What am I going to do?" My anger is mixed with despair. I stand with my head dropped and my shoulders sagging in defeat. Max comes to me from behind and places his hands on my shoulders.

"Go pack you and Charley a bag for a few days. I'll take you both out to the farm. You can stay with Mom and Dad until you decide what you want to do. Just take a few days before you make any major life decisions." Max turns me around to look at him.

"But I need to find a job tomorrow."

"You can wait a few days before you do that. I know you have always been prepared in case something ever happened to your job. Take advantage of that and don't rush into anything. Go pack. I'll run over and get Charley."

Max pushes me toward the hall and turns to leave. What he says makes sense. I don't need to rush into any big job decisions. I need to look at everything and decide where the best place for us will be. Maybe Charley and I should consider moving somewhere else. Big decisions need to take a little time. Plus, there is no way I can stay here tonight, so going out to the farm to see Kathleen and Jack may be the best thing for us.

I quickly throw some clothes in our bags. I think about packing some toys for Charley but decide against it. The child has a full toy box in her room at the farm. Kathleen went all out in decorating one of their spare rooms when Charley was born. She wanted it to be Charley's room and she keeps it stocked with anything a little girl might like. Jack jokes all the time that Charley may be the only grandchild they ever have because Max won't settle down with anyone. I'm just grateful they love my daughter. Since Charley has no family on my side, it has been a blessing for her to have Max's parents be the grandparents that my mom and dad can't be.

Just when I walk back into the living room with our bags, Max walks in carrying Charley. I don't know what they have been saying but Charley is laughing at Max. She jumps down when she sees me, running to give me a hug.

"Uncle Max says we're going to the farm to stay. I get to see Papa and Mums!" My little one jumps up and down as she talks.

Charley suddenly pulls at the bottom of my shirt. "Mommy! What about Daddy? We won't be here tonight when he gets home. He won't know where we are! We can't leave!" Charley's voice gets more anxious as she talks. I feel the tears coming back as I look to Max for a way to answer her. Max squats to be at eye level with her.

"It will be okay, Munchkin. Your daddy has some work that he has to take care of so he can't come out for a few days anyway. He won't mind you staying over with Papa and Mums. Why don't you go get the doll your daddy gave you and bring it with you?" I let out a huge breath. *Thank you Max*. I let him know without words how appreciative I am for him handling that. Hopefully that will keep Charley calm until I can figure out how we are going to handle her spending time with her father.

Charley seems to calm but you can see sadness in

her eyes. "Okay. I'm going to miss him. I'll just talk to him on the phone every night." She runs to her room to get her doll. Max and I share a look that tells me I will have to make that happen for her whether I want to or not.

As soon as Charley comes back into the living room, Max picks up our bags and nudges us toward the door. "Come on ladies. I called Papa and Mums and they're holding dinner for us. Let's get on the road."

Charley holds Max's hand as they head out the door. I lag behind while locking up the apartment.

"Hey, Gemma, toss me your keys so I can get Charley's car seat," Max calls out to me.

Even though I know I should take my own vehicle, the thought of not having to drive right now appeals to me. Max has Charley buckled into it in no time. I settle in the front seat as Max walks around to get into the truck.

Knowing that Tiba will be concerned about me, I pull out my phone to send her a quick text. Opening the screen, I see multiple missed calls from Raef. He has left voicemails and sent text messages. Deciding that I am not ready to hear or see anything from him, I ignore them and pull up Tiba instead.

Me: Charley & I are going to spend a few days at Jack & Kathleen's. I'll talk to you when we get back.

I hit send. It's only a few seconds before I get a response.

Tiba: Okay. Call me when you feel like it. It's all going to be okay. Love you!

I love Tiba like a sister and I know she worries about me but I just don't think I want to talk to her for a few days. She will only try to convince me to talk to Raef. Even so, I don't want to hurt her feeling so I just send a simple *Love you too*.

By this time Max has us on the road to his parents' house. The ride to the farm usually only takes about half an hour. Charley rattles to Max about something, so I am able to let my mind wander as I watch the scenery. Whether I like it or not, my mind wanders to Raef. I know I will eventually have to talk to him. I just can't do that until I pull myself together. Hopefully a few days with Kathleen will help me do just that.

CHAPTER SIXTEEN

RAEF

TRAFFIC COMING OUT OF THE city turned out to be a nightmare. I should have known considering the time of day. The drive to Gemma's apartment takes much longer than I had hoped. I continue to attempt to reach her the entire trip, but no answer. I can also see that she hasn't read the text messages. Maybe it's better this way. I can talk to her in person and she can see the truth in my eyes. Over the phone she would doubt me.

The first thing I notice when I pull into the parking lot of the apartment complex is Gemma's car. Relief floods through me. She's home. I didn't realize that I had been subconsciously worried she might not be here. This is good news. I can get this entire mess straightened out tonight. I quickly park next to her car and jump out. *When we are engaged, I am getting her a new vehicle and out of this old thing.* But then I chastise myself for even thinking about her car at a time like this.

Gemma had given me a key to the apartment earlier this week, but with the circumstances I feel it might be better to knock so that's what I do. I wait. No answer so I knock again. Again I wait. No answer and no sounds coming from inside. Pulling out my key, I let myself in. The lights are off and it appears no one is here. I run through each room calling for Gemma and Charlotte. Neither answer because neither are here. *Where can they be? Her car is here.*

Alexis. The babysitter. That has to be where they are. Maybe Gemma just got here and is still over there with Charlotte. Making quick work of locking the apartment, I run—literally run—to Alexis's apartment and knock on her door. It is only a few seconds before she opens the door. She looks shocked to see me.

"Oh, hey, Raef. Did Charley forget something?" Alexis asks.

"I was looking for Gemma and Charlotte. I thought they may still be here since they aren't at home and Gem's car is in the lot."

"I haven't seen Gemma today. Max picked Charley up some time ago. He didn't mention they were going anywhere but maybe they went to eat or something. He did say that Charley wouldn't be here for a few days." Despair fills me again. It must be apparent to Alexis because she quickly asks, "Raef, are you okay? You look like you might pass out." She frowns with concern.

"I'm not okay but I will be. I have to find Gemma to straighten out a huge misunderstanding. Sorry to bother you."

I head toward my vehicle. I could ask Alexis for Max's phone number, but that might be awkward for her. Plus, if Gem is with him, she probably wouldn't let him answer my call anyway. I will just have to locate them on my own. I know most of the decent places to eat in this town. They shouldn't be too hard to find. At least that's what I tell myself as I head out of the parking lot.

I drive by every place I can think of and still don't spot Max's truck. Back at the apartment parking lot, nothing has changed. Gemma's car is still there, Max's truck is not there and there are no lights on in the apartment. I get out and do one more check inside the apartment before I head out again. For a brief moment I contemplate going back and asking Alexis for that phone number but decide against it. There is one more thing I haven't tried.

Pulling out my phone, I look up Tiba's number and hit dial. While I wait for her to answer, I find myself sending up a quick prayer.

God, if you are really up there please help me find Gemma. Please don't let me lose her again.

I am not an overly religious person but I was brought up Catholic and know I need all the help I can get right now.

"Hello?" Tiba answers with a question in her voice.

If this was your doings, God, then thank you!!!

"Tiba, this is Raef." I know that she is probably very angry with me, so I feel like I need to give her a moment before I jump into trying to find out where Gemma is.

"Oh. Hey, Raef. Are you calling to make sure I got your message about being out of work?" I can hear a bit of anger in her voice but not what I would have expected considering the situation.

"Tiba, you have to believe me. That was not me. It was all my father. He's trying to drive Gemma away from me. I own the salon now so there is nothing to worry about with your job. I just need a few days to get everything straight."

I hold my breath hoping she will believe me because I know otherwise there will be no chance of finding out anything about Gemma. I hear a sigh on the other end and take that as a good sign.

"I didn't think it was you, Raef. I even told Gemma that, but she thinks it was you. Have you seen her yet? She was pretty upset with you when we left the shop earlier."

"No, I haven't seen her. She won't answer my calls or read my texts. I've been by the apartment but she and Charlotte aren't there. I was hoping you might know where they are." I am not really sure how fast those words came out of my mouth but it was fast enough that I hope Tiba understood all of them.

"She texted me about an hour ago. She and Charley are going to spend a few days out at Max's parents' farm. I hoped she had talked to you before she left." Relief floods through me for a second time tonight. I feel so much better just knowing where they are.

"Do you know where the Greenwood's live? I want to head out there." I pace in the parking lot.

"I'll text you the address, but Raef, I don't think you should go tonight. Wait until tomorrow." Tiba seems a little hesitant, but she also seems very sincere.

"Why would I wait? I need to get to her and let her know this wasn't anything to do with me." My voice is getting more anxious and my pacing more furious.

"Gemma was really, really upset when she left. If she went out to the farm, Kathleen will have a real calming effect on her and Kathleen will more than likely tell her the same thing I did, which was to talk to you. Give her a little time, Raef. I think it will all work out better if you wait until tomorrow evening to go out there." Listening to Tiba, I am so thankful that Gemma has such a good friend. It's obvious that Tiba understands how Gemma thinks. It's equally clear how much she cares for her friend.

"Even though I don't want to, I will do it your way and wait. Thank you, Tiba. Thanks for believing in me and thanks for being such a good friend to Gemma." I head toward my car since I know I am now headed back into the city.

"No problem. Just don't ever hurt my girl, Raef. I'd have to hunt you down." I can hear the smile in Tiba's cheeky comment. For the first time since my dad dropped the news of what he had done, I smile.

"No worries, Tiba. I don't plan to hurt her. Once we get this all straightened out, the only thing I plan to do is make her my wife."

"Perfect." Tiba disconnects the call and I toss my phone into the other seat of my car. I sit for a few moments while I absorb what Tiba has told me.

It seems that Gemma has gotten even closer to the Greenwoods over the years we were apart. That would make sense, since her own parents are gone. I would imagine they are also very close to Charlotte. It is strange to realize that the Greenwoods most likely act as grandparents to my daughter while my own parents don't even know about her. Well, my mother doesn't know about her. It seems my father does and obviously has for some time. My mind is made up as to where I am going tonight. It's time for my mother to know she is a grandmother. Hitting the phone button on my car, I dial my mom's phone.

"Well hello, Raeford." My mom answers on the first ring with her typical response. Why she has to continue to call me Raeford is beyond me. She knows I hate it but she does it all of the time.

"Hey, Mom, I want to drop by and see you tonight if that's okay."

"Sure you can, Son! I'm anxious to see you now that we are back home from our trip." Mom's voice always makes me feel a little better about things and this time is no exception.

"I'll be there in about an hour or so. And Mom—" I hesitate because I don't want to raise any questions with her, "Is Dad going to be there?" I hope she doesn't hear the anger in my voice. Just saying the word *Dad* right now is not pleasant for me.

"No, you won't get to see him tonight. He and some friends decided to go to the country club for dinner. You know how he is when he gets back from a trip. They will be there until the club bar closes." Mom chuckles. I let out the breath I was holding and end the call, telling my mother that I will be there shortly.

As I drive back to the city, my thoughts wander to Gemma. It is no surprise she immediately believed I would do something to hurt her. I mean, I did hurt her once. I had hoped this last week had shown her I would never do that again. In all reasonableness though, a week isn't a very long time.

I decide to make a call to Daniel to tell him what has happened. Since he handled everything with my purchase of the salons, I need to get him involved on how to proceed with getting this mess straight. Daniel answers and I fill him in on the happenings of the last several hours. I thought he would be more surprised by our father's actions than he is but he doesn't seem shocked at all. He is more shocked by the fact that I walked out and quit my job. By the time we end the call, we have everything planned to get the business side of things handled with the salons.

Mom must have been watching for me because she meets me on the porch with open arms. I walk into a welcomed hug from the woman who always makes everything better. The comfort of her arms is almost overwhelming after the day I have endured. I find myself almost at the breaking point. Knowing I have much that I need to tell her, I pull myself back from my mom's arms.

"Raeford, you look like death warmed over, Son. What's wrong?" Leave it to my mother to be blunt about things. Of course, I am sure I do look pretty rough. Hours of running my hands through my hair in frustration has probably made it a sight to see.

"Thanks, Mom. Here I was about to tell you how beautiful you are. And please don't call me Raeford." Mom swats me on the arm as we head in to the living room.

"Now, now. You know that is your name so I will call you that whenever I please." Mom sits next to me on the sofa. "And you can call me beautiful any time you want to, Son. You know that." She flashes me one of those classic Ruth Alvero smiles. My mother is truly a beautiful woman inside and out.

"Mom, I have some things to tell you. Things that will surprise you but that I hope will make you happy. At least, I hope you will be happy for me." I look up and see the questions on her face. My mom has always tried to be involved with her children, so I know she is wondering what I could be about to tell her. I decide to forge on without waiting for her response.

"Do you remember Gemma Warren? The girl I dated several years ago?" Mom nods briefly. "Well,

Gemma and I are back together again. I plan to make her my wife. I have a daughter with her named Charlotte. She is four years old." Ripping off the bandage is usually the best way, so I just throw it out there for her to hear. I can see the shock on her face. Obviously my father did not tell her what he knew. I show my mother the screensaver picture of Charlotte on my phone.

"Oh my goodness! I am a grandmother!" Tears form in my mother's eyes as she looks at the picture.

"Yes, you are a grandmother. To a beautiful little girl that looks just like Marie did as a child. I can't wait for you to meet her." Tears stream down her face. "Are those good tears Mom?"

She grabs me into a tight hug. "Oh yes, they are good tears. I'm so happy." She stills suddenly and backs away to look at me again. "Are you back together just for the child or do you really love her?"

"I love her, Mom. I love her more than anything. Well, anything but Charlotte. I should have never left her to begin with but that was *my father's* fault." I growl out the words *my father* to her. I see her brow furrow as she looks at me.

"What has happened with you and your father? Since everything was fine when he left here earlier, I'm assuming that something happened today."

Feeling confined, I begin to pace the room. I tell her everything that has happened. I start with how he talked me into leaving Gemma five years ago. I tell her about seeing Gemma again, finding out about Charlotte and how wonderful things have been with us as a family. I tell her about all that happened today and how he acted at the office, about what he did to try to drive Gemma away from me. I end with how I have quit my job and that I had already purchased the salons personally from the company. As I finish with everything, I stop and look at her for the first time. I notice she isn't looking at me. We both are quiet for a few moments before she finally raises her head and begins to speak.

"Oh, Raef. I was so hoping nothing like this would happen with you. You have always been so close to your father. I was hoping you would never have to see this side of him."

"What do you mean?" The worry is obvious on my mother's face.

"Your father gets what he wants no matter who may be hurt in the process. You grew up being his little shadow, always wanting to be just like him. When Charles realized your brother wasn't going to cave to his wishes and do exactly what your father had planned for him, Charles attached himself to you. You never questioned your father on anything. You just blindly followed him and Charles jumped at that connection. To him, he finally had a son that was "his" to do with as he pleased. It concerned me a little, but you had such a good honest heart that I didn't feel I needed to intervene." My mother pauses at this point. She looks as if she is considering what more to say.

"I don't understand what you're saying, Mom. Dad has never acted like this before and I have worked with him for quite some time now."

My mother gives me a small smile, shrouded with sadness. Her expression grips my heart. She looks almost defeated. It is a look I have never seen on her before.

"Charles has hidden his true side from you well. We all have. Daniel and Marie don't really discuss their relationship with their father do they?" Realizing what she says is true, I shake my head. "Exactly. They know how close you are with your father so they don't bring up the fact that they have no relationship with him. He has not been a father to them. Somewhere along the way, the ruthlessness of business took over his heart and he became ruthless in all areas of his life. He is no longer the man I married."

A tear slides down my mother's cheek. It breaks my heart to see her in such despair. I sit beside her on the couch and pull her into a hug. She continues to speak as I hold her.

"I know you three kids have always wondered why my father left his estate to you instead of me. The reason is your father. When your father founded Alvero & Alvero with your uncle, he tried to take over my father's company. He didn't even discuss it with me; he just made a vicious attack. Dexter told me what was happening. Dex & I were able to warn my father in enough time for him to fend off the takeover. Charles was furious with both of us and things have never been the same since then. Charles never apologized to your Gramps nor to me. My father was civil to Charles for my sake but he never forgave him for his actions. He told me about his will sometime after that time. He felt he couldn't leave me his estate because Charles would have his hands on it. Instead, he opened an account for me that your father has never known about. It has ironclad documents that will not allow Charles to have any of it if something should happen to me. That was his way of taking care of me. Leaving his estate to the three of you was my father's way of making sure your father could not touch anything that had been his." My mother's words continue to shock me. How could I have not known any of this?

"Why hasn't anyone told me any of this before?" I question my mother. If I had known this, would it have changed any of my previous decisions?

"I thought about talking to you several times over the last few years but things seemed to be going so well for you. With Charles planning to back out of the company and retire, I honestly thought you might be able to avoid having to experience this side of him. I didn't know that you had a child or I would have told you everything. I am so sorry, Raef. I feel this is all my fault." The guilt is evident in Mom's voice.

"It's not your fault, Mom. It's mine. I blindly listened to Dad. I have no excuse other than being young and ambitious. I can't change the past but I can change my future. Dad will not convince me to walk away from Gemma and Charlotte now." My voice is full of the conviction I feel. I kiss the top of my mother's head and pull away from her. "I do have one question though, Mom. Why do you stay with him? If Dad is like this with everyone, why haven't you left him?"

Mom ducks her head as she speaks. "I still love him, Raef. I keep hoping that once he walks away from the company, maybe he will become the young Charles Alvero again. The Charles I married." Mom looks up at me with her eyes bright with tears. They are the same color blue as mine and they shine brightly, full of love. Love I know is not only for me but for my father.

"I understand, Mom. I had no idea how strong love really was until I found Gemma again. Then I realized I never stopped loving her. These last few years I have just been existing. Work was the only life I've had.

Being with her again has shown me what living really is. I have to fix what Dad has created so Gemma, Charlotte and I can begin our lives together." I stand to leave, extending my hand to my mother. She takes my hand, standing also. I give her one more hug as we turn to walk to the door.

"Fix it, Raef. I know you want to work for Alvero & Alvero, but if having your family means you have to walk away from the company, then do it. Walk away. And bring those two to see me very soon. I can't wait to meet my granddaughter!"

"Don't worry, Mom. Once I get this all straightened out, you will be the first person we visit." I give her a quick kiss on the cheek as I open the door. "I love you, Mom. Thanks for the talk."

"I love you too, Raef." One thing I know for certain in my life is when my mother says those words, she absolutely means them. I have never had to doubt the love of my mother. She is the rock of our family, always showing each of us kids her love.

Thinking about everything my mother has just told me, I head back to my apartment. Knowing all of this makes it clear to me that working with my father is no longer an option. My decision to walk away from Alvero & Alvero today is for the best. Tomorrow I will tender my official resignation. I will never put my career before Gemma and Charlotte again. That one decision I made five years ago was a lesson learned the hard way. I have always thought I was a carbon copy of my father but tonight it has become clear to me that I am much more like my mother and grandfather. Tomorrow will be the first day in the life I truly want for myself.

CHAPTER SEVENTEEN

GEMMA

AFTER A RESTLESS NIGHT, I venture into the kitchen in search of coffee. I find not only coffee but also Kathleen. She looks ready to talk which is exactly what I was expecting. Kathleen has always given me time to process things on my terms but then she is available to talk when I need her. She always says that a person needs time to think but if they keep things inside too long they will think too much and that isn't a good thing. Since the loss of my mom, I have always known that I can come to Kathleen for great advice.

"Good morning, Gemma. I hope you were able to get some rest last night." Kathleen greats me with a hug.

"Not much, but I really didn't expect to rest. Too much on my mind. Where's Charley?" I look around the room as I pour myself a cup of coffee. Kathleen already has a coffee cup waiting for me.

"Jack took her out riding this morning. You know he loves to get her on a horse anytime he can. I thought it would be a good idea so you and I could have a few moments alone this morning."

Just as I expected, Kathleen is ready to hear the

story. I don't mind because I really need someone to talk to right now. Jack & Kathleen have a wonderful marriage, much like my parents did. I want that type of future, not only for me, but also for Charley. If anyone can give me the advice I need, it will be Kathleen.

"I'm glad. She enjoys being with Jack." I smile as I think about Charley and her 'Papa' as she calls him.

"Jack enjoys her just as much. She will always be our first grandchild. I hope you know that. Of course, at the rate Max is going with women, Charley may be our only one." I can't help but chuckle at the expression on Kathleen's face. It is running joke in this house about Max and his disregard for settling down with one woman.

"Oh don't worry. Max will settle down one day when he finds the right woman. I'm sure you'll have a passel of grandchildren to fill the house one day."

"I hope so! That boy is something else. I just hope that when he does find the right one she knocks him off his feet!" Kathleen is so funny when she talks about Max. I can't help but chuckle again. Even when I feel terrible, this woman can always make me smile. "Let's you and I go sit on the porch and talk, Gemma. You look like you could use an ear this morning," Kathleen prompts me to move toward the door.

The two of us move to the porch and sit in the large rocking chairs Kathleen keeps there. The view from the front porch is spectacular. Jack and Kathleen live north of Granier so they are out of the swamplands. Their house is on the edge of their property at the top of a small hill. It overlooks the land they own with a gorgeous view of the farm. Kathleen once told me she knew the moment she stepped on this spot of land this would be where they made their home. This porch has been a very calming spot for me over the years since I lost my parents.

Kathleen and I sit quietly. I know I am postponing the conversation, but the moment seems too peaceful to disturb. My mind drifts to Raef. I can't help but wonder what he is thinking. What if he really didn't have anything to do with closing the salon? Could I have it all wrong? I shake my head as if that will clear my thoughts. Needless to say, it does no good. My rocking slows and Kathleen obviously picks up on my mood change. She breaks the silence.

"So, Max seems to think that Raef had nothing to do with what happened. Considering how much Max has hated that boy for the last five years, he must have a good reason to believe Raef wasn't behind this." Kathleen has never been one to dance around a subject. When she speaks, she always jumps right to the heart of things.

"I just don't know. At first I was just so hurt and angry that I thought it had to be him just because he had hurt me before. Now, I just don't know. Since he's been back in my life, he's acted like he really wants to be with me. Plus, Charley has him wrapped around her little finger. I don't know what to think. Maybe he just decided he didn't want to be with us after all." That is my greatest fear. I just haven't admitted it to myself in the last 24 hours. I don't know if my heart can survive life without Raef again.

"Oh honey, I don't believe that. And I definitely don't believe he would walk away from Charley. I haven't seen the two of you together but Max has told me how enthralled Raef became with her the first night he met her."

"But what does Max really know? He only knows what he saw that first night. Everything else is simply things I have told him. Maybe I was reading everything wrong. Maybe I was just seeing what I wanted to see." I stand and walk to the end of porch. Leaning against the post, I cross my arms across my chest and stare out towards the wooded section of the property. Kathleen walks over to put her arm around me.

"Honey, Max has always been able to read you like a book. He just knows. I always said that he never could have had a brother or sister he knew any better than he knew you. I really feel that you need to just sit down and talk to Raef. How do you think Jack and I have made it all these years? We talk. Things happen and one of us will assume the worst about the other, but we sit down and talk about it. That way we know exactly what the other is thinking."

We stand in silence for a bit before we see two horses headed our way. Jack and Charley are still a good distance away but are headed toward the house. Charley is riding her horse, Blue. Jack bought the older horse for Charley when she was just a baby. He said he knew the moment he laid eyes on the horse that he was meant for Charley. I laughed at him at the time but he was right. Since she was old enough to walk, she has bonded with that horse. He is older and very gentle, especially when Charley is riding him.

"You're right, Kathleen. I think I'm just scared." I turn to look at Kathleen. "What if he rejects me again? I don't know if I can handle it a second time, especially now that I have Charley."

Tears spill from my eyes and I hastily wipe them away. The tears make me angry at myself. I want to be stronger, but I can't seem to be where Raef is concerned. His rejection would break me and I know it. That fear is why I ran last night.

Kathleen pulls me into her arms for a tight hug. More tears flow as she holds me and lets me cry. "Gemma, you know that I will always be honest with you don't you?" Kathleen pulls away, holding my shoulders and looking straight into my eyes.

"Of course I know that. You always have been."

"Then talk to that boy. I don't believe he is going to reject you or Charley. But, if I am wrong and he does, you are strong. You can get through it. You are the strongest girl I know. So pull up your big girl panties and talk to Raef. Not only for you, but for Charley." Kathleen hugs me again and heads off the porch to meet Jack and Charley.

Still standing on the porch, I watch the interaction between my daughter and the two people she knows as grandparents. My tears dry and I think about the words Kathleen had spoken to me. She's right. I am strong. No matter what, I will survive.

My mind is made up; I will talk to Raef. It isn't fair to him or to Charley for me to hide from him. Coming here to the farm always clears my head. Maybe it is the fresh air or maybe it is just being with Kathleen and Jack. The two are my surrogate parents and have taken that role seriously. I smile as I watch Charley tell Kathleen all about her ride. Her little voice carries and I can hear bits and pieces of what she is saying. She's so happy when she's here. I really must bring her out here more often.

I decide to give Kathleen and Jack a little more alone time with Charley as I turn to head into the house. It's time to get our things ready to head back into town. We'll spend the day here at the farm and then

I'll see if either Jack or Kathleen can take us home. Just as I am about to go into the house, I notice dust in the distance. Expecting it to be Max, I head on into the house with the thought that maybe Charley and I can just catch a ride back to town with him.

CHAPTER EIGHTEEN

RAEF

KNOWING IT WOULD BE POINTLESS to even try to sleep, I don't bother to go to bed. Instead I type out my resignation letter, copy the documents I need from the salon purchase and watch the clock. When daylight is nears, I shower and head to the office.

No one is in the building other than security, so getting to my office is uneventful. I enter my office and look around. There really isn't much for me to pack. It saddens me to realize how few personal items I have here. I gather my framed college degrees and the few college awards I have displayed. I spend some time going through my desk to make sure I leave nothing personal behind. I look back at my office one more time before turning off the light. Walking out, I close the door on that chapter of my life.

Since it is still early, I take a few minutes to take the box of things to my car. I retrieve my resignation letter from my car and head to my father's office. He won't be here this early which is fine with me. I have no desire to see him.

Heading into the building once more, I take the elevator to the top floor. The only offices on that level are those of my father and Uncle Dex. It is quiet when I get off the elevator, but I see the light on in my uncle's office. I quickly leave my resignation letter and salon purchase documents on my father's assistant's desk.

When I walk into my uncle's office, he looks up from his desk in surprise.

"Hello, Raef. What has you up here this early in the morning?"

"I had to leave some things for my father. I was shocked to see you here." Uncle Dex never gets to the office this early.

"I decided I wanted to play golf today. I came in early to finish up a few things that couldn't wait." Uncle Dex looks closely at my expression. "What's going on, Raef?"

"I just left my resignation letter for my father. I am leaving Alvero & Alvero."

"Leaving? Why? Do you have another job?" Uncle Dex's confusion is apparent. Everyone here knows that I am supposed to move into my father's position soon.

"No. Suffice it to say, my father is the reason I am leaving." I tell Uncle Dex about the things my father has done, from the first time with Gemma to yesterday. Like my mother, he doesn't look surprised.

"I hate to hear this. My brother can be quite the asshole. I just thought you were off limits to him. I am thrilled to hear I have a great-niece though." Uncle Dex comes around his desk to hug me. Unlike my father, Dex has always been one to show affection. "I hate to lose you here, but this is the right thing for you to do."

Uncle Dex and I talk for a few more minutes. I

show him pictures of Charlotte and Gemma on my phone. He assures me he will help me find another job and I promise I will bring Gemma and Charlotte to meet him soon.

The last thing I have to do before leaving the office for the last time is meet with my assistant, Ashley. Regardless of what my father had told me of his plans for me to be with Ashley, I can't help but feel sorry for her. I have no idea if she will have a job here any longer.

"Good morning, Raef." Ashley greets me when I enter her office.

"Morning, Ashley. Can we talk?"

"Of course. Do you want me to come in your office?" She starts to get up from her desk.

"No. Let's do this here." I sit in front of her desk.

Deciding not to hide anything, I tell her about my resignation and the things my father told me about his plans for us. The horror on her face tells me that she knew nothing of his plans.

"Oh no, Raef! You have to believe I didn't know. I work here because I want to. Why would your father even think we would be together?"

"My father's mind obviously doesn't work like most. It seems he has one devious plan after another." I give her a quick run-down of the events that led to my resignation. I end with telling her about Charlotte.

Knowing my father will be in the office soon, I end my conversation with Ashley. I suggest she visit Uncle Dex to see if he can help her move to another position in the company. Who knows? If I can find another job soon, maybe I can bring her over with me.

My first stop after leaving Alvero & Alvero is the

salon in Granier. I meet a locksmith and have the locks changed. I had contacted employees of the other four salons last night and made sure they knew they weren't closing. They were in charge of changing the locks at each of their locations this morning.

Tiba had seemed interested in a few days off, so I didn't call her this morning to come to the shop. I will call her after I see Gemma and see if I can drop her new key off to her then. She can decide when she wants to return. At least I know my father won't have access to any of the locations. The purchase documents are ironclad and board approved so he has no choice but to accept them.

As soon as the locksmith finishes his work, I head out of town. Tiba had told me to give Gemma some time but I am not going to wait any longer. The need to see her is too strong. When I turn onto the gravel road on the Greenwood's property I begin to feel a little better. I am close to Gemma. I just hope she will talk to me.

My main worry is whether or not Jack Greenwood will allow me to stay on his property and see her. I know that he is like a father to Gemma and will most certainly protect her like a father would. I guess it will just depend on what Gemma and Max have told him about me. I am sure the fact that I was absent for five years won't weigh in my favor.

As I approach the house, I see Charlotte outside with two adults who must be Jack & Kathleen Greenwood. There are also two horses being held by the older man. Charlotte looks like she is telling quite a story with arms flying everywhere while she jumps around the horses. Despite my worries, I can't help but smile at my daughter. She is quite the little live wire.

I park my car behind the other vehicles in the driveway. The adults have been watching my car approach but Charlotte hasn't noticed it yet. I get out and walk in their direction. I look around but don't see Gemma anywhere. I assume she is inside the house. Charlotte seems to notice that the adults are no longer paying attention to her and she looks toward where they are looking. When she sees me walking her direction she takes off running toward me shouting, "DADDY!"

As Charlotte reaches me, I drop to my knee to grab her in a hug. She wraps her little arms around my neck so tightly I almost cry. Her hugs are the best and I suddenly have the feeling that everything is going to be just fine. Amazing what a hug can make you feel, especially coming from a four-year old.

"I missed you sooooo much Daddy!" Charlotte says as she is still wrapped around me. I stand with her in my arms and continue my walk toward the Greenwoods.

"I missed you too, Charlotte. I missed you very much. But I'm here now. Why don't you introduce me to these nice people?" I stand before the Greenwoods with Charlotte in my arms.

"This is my Papa and Mums," Charlotte says as she points to the two people staring at me. "And this is my Daddy." Charlotte points at me while still looking at Jack and Kathleen Greenwood. Neither make a move so I know that I will have to initiate this conversation. Holding Charlotte with one arm and, I extend my other hand toward Jack Greenwood.

"Hello Mr. and Mrs. Greenwood. I'm Raef Alvero. I was hoping to speak with Gemma." As I stand awkwardly with my hand still extended and two sets of eyes boring into mine, Jack Greenwood slowly lifts his hand to shake mine. I am relieved as I shake his hand. He doesn't speak but his wife does.

"Nice to meet you, Raef." Kathleen Greenwood pulls me into a hug. After pulling back, she takes Charlotte from my arms and tilts her head toward the house saying, "She's inside. Go ahead on in. Charley and I are going to help Papa tend to these horses, aren't we, Charley?"

Charlotte looks from me to Kathleen and back to me. She nods and says, "Okay, but don't leave before I get through, Daddy."

I smile at my precious daughter. "I just need a little time to talk to your momma and then I'll come back out and find you." I lean over and give her a quick kiss on the cheek before looking back at the Greenwoods. "Thank you."

As I turn and begin to walk toward the house I hear Jack Greenwood call, "Alvero!" I stop walking and slowly turn toward him, holding my breath as I do.

"That girl is like a daughter to me. Don't you hurt her." He glares at me as he speaks.

"Don't worry, sir. I don't plan on it." I turn back toward the house and begin walking again. I hear Kathleen Greenwood in the background berating her husband for his words. I can't help but smile. I have one of them on my side.

When I enter the house, I notice the open floor-plan. It is a beautiful home, not too large but not small by any means. I can see throughout the entire living area and into the kitchen/dining area.

"Gemma," I call in a voice that isn't too loud but hopefully loud enough for her to hear me. Being impatient, I don't give time for a response before

I call out again, "Gemma." I was a little louder this time. Hearing sounds coming from the right side of the house, I turn and walk that direction.

At the moment I am about to enter the hall to the right, Gemma steps out of a room. Her expression is one of shock. It's obvious she didn't expect me to find her here. There is also fear in her eyes. I don't like the fear I see. I never want her to feel fearful where I am concerned.

"Raef, what are you doing here?" Gemma asks me quietly. I want to pull her into my arms but I know we have to talk before I can do that. Still, I take a few steps closer to her. The need to be close to her is great.

"I came—" I step even closer to her but she steps back a step. That one step drives a knife through my heart. What if she won't believe me? I will just have to fight even harder for her. "Let's go sit and talk Gemma." I tilt my head toward the living area.

Gemma doesn't answer, but she does walk by me and heads into the living area. She doesn't stop there, but continues on to the kitchen. Like a gracious hostess she asks, "Would you like anything to drink?" I shake my head no so she sits in a chair at the table, her head down. I follow suit sitting across from her.

"Gemma, look at me please." She raises her eyes to mine. There is fear and sadness in them. "Gemma, I had nothing to do with what happened yesterday. My father set it up to make you think it was me." I see a glimmer of hope in her eyes for just a moment. I press on.

"I learned a lot about my father yesterday. Things I never knew. He played me five years ago when he talked me into breaking things off with you. Then he found out about Charlotte some time ago but never told me. He pulled this stunt yesterday to keep you away from me. He actually cut their vacation short. He thought I would walk away again. I didn't though and I won't." I stop for a moment to try to read her. The hope is back and her eyes are glassy like tears are forming.

"My father has played me for a long time now without me realizing it. Those days are over now. I resigned from Alvero & Alvero this morning. I have cleaned out my office and will not return."

Gemma's expression changes a bit as we sit in silence. I want to give her a few moments to absorb what I have said so far. She still doesn't say anything so I continue.

"I wanted to come to you as soon as my father told me what he was doing. I drove out to Granier as fast as I could but you were already gone. I didn't know what to do so I called Tiba. She told me you were out here and to give you some time. I gave you last night, but I couldn't wait any longer. I had to get to you and make sure you knew the truth." A tear falls down Gemma's cheek.

"You quit your job? Your dad closed my shop? I don't understand, Raef. Why would he do that?" I am so relieved to hear her speak that I can't help myself. I reach across the table and take her hand between my hands. Touching her is like an electrical current going through my body.

"When I found out you were staying here at the farm I didn't know what to do. I didn't want to go back to my apartment in the city alone, so I visited my mother. She was home alone and I needed to talk to someone. I told her everything that happened yesterday and to my surprise, she wasn't shocked by any of it. It seems that my father can be an evil man when things don't happen the way he wants them to. I am obviously the only one who had not figured that out. It seems that I have always done what he wanted so there was no reason for me to see that side of him. But boy did I ever see it yesterday. I quit my job because I can't work with my father any longer. I can't work with the man I saw yesterday. And I surely can't work with anyone that will try to keep me away from you and Charlotte. There's nothing in this world more important than the two of you." I move to the chair next to Gemma, all the while holding her hand. I can't let that connection go and I have to be closer to her. She watches me, still wary.

"I wanted this to be a wedding present for you, Gemma, but with all that's happened, I can't wait." Her mouth drops open at the words wedding present. She looks confused as I continue. "I purchased the five salons my father planned to close. The board approved the purchase while he was gone because it would be ridiculous not to. I offered them a sum of money for five businesses that, if closed, would provide them nothing. The salons are in your name as owner. Your salon and four others are yours, Gemma. All yours. You can choose to do with them whatever you want. You didn't lose your job yesterday, baby; you own the place. My father was playing a vicious game—one he didn't win."

Gemma stares at me for the longest moment. I try to read her but I can't seem to. I see all sorts of emotions in her but the biggest of the moment seems to be shock.

"I don't know how to run salons, Raef. Why would

you buy them for me? I am so confused. What does all of this mean?" Gemma pulls her hand back from mine and I feel the loss of her touch immediately. I can't handle that feeling so I reach for her hand and take it in mine again. I half expect her to pull away but she doesn't. I sigh in relief.

"What this means is that I love you, Gemma. Nothing, not even my father, is going to take you away from me again. I bought the salons because I knew my father would close them. I couldn't make the numbers work enough for a company as big as Alvero & Alvero to hang on to them. I wanted them to be your wedding present, but dear old dad ruined that. And you do know how to run salons. The shop that you and Tiba run is the only one of the five that consistently turns a profit. But we will work out all of the details on how you want to handle them all later. Right now I just want you to know I love you and you have a job." I take one hand and reach into my pocket to pull out the new key. I hold it out to her. "Here is the new key to your shop. I had the locks changed this morning so my father wouldn't be able to gain access. I'll drop Tiba's key off on my way back through Granier."

Gemma hesitantly reaches out and takes the key. She stares at it like it is a treasure then looks back up at me. Tears cover her face. I can't help myself as I reach out to wipe her tears away. She still hasn't said anything so I am not sure if she believes me or not. I can't stand it any longer, I have to know what she is thinking.

"Gemma, do you believe me? Do you see how much I love you?" I plead with her. She seems to be at war with how to respond. Her hesitancy scares me.

"I believe you, Raef, but this is all so much to take in. I don't know what to think or do. It's just over-whelming. I need time to think and process it all. So much has happened in the last couple of weeks. Can you give me time?" The look Gemma gives me is hopeful but I can still see fear in her eyes. I don't want to give her time but I know I can't push her.

"I love you, Gemma, and I love Charlotte. If time is what you need, then I will give you time. All I ask is that you please not take too much time. If I don't hear from you within a couple of days, I will be back."

I stand, still holding her hand. I don't want to leave but I know I have to. If I stay, all she has to do is get Jack Greenwood involved and I really won't have a choice. As close as she is to the Greenwoods, I don't want to do something to make them hate me. I need them on my side.

Pulling my hand from hers, I bend down and place my hands on each side of her face. Knowing I won't see her for a few days, I can't help but taste her one time before I leave. I lean in and kiss her with all of the love I am feeling. She doesn't respond for a moment but then she kisses me back. Ending the kiss, I place my forehead against hers.

"I love you, Gemma." I place one more quick kiss on her lips before I walk away. As much as I want to turn and look back, I don't. Gemma has to decide that she wants me as much as I want her.

Knowing that I need to see Charlotte before I leave, I head to the barn. Charlotte is helping Jack Green-wood brush a horse. I stand quietly and watch them. He is definitely good with my daughter. I think of my own father. He will never be the grandfather to Charlotte that this man is. As I step forward, the two hear me.

"Hey, Daddy! This is my horse. His name is Blue. Papa lets me help brush him. He says that if I have a horse, I have to take care of him. Right, Papa?" Charlotte looks at the man she calls Papa.

"That's right, little one." He ruffles her hair before he looks back to me. His expression is enough to let me know that he wants to know what happened inside his house.

"That is a good thing to learn, Charlotte. I'm glad your Papa is teaching you to take care of things you have. One day you will have to show me how he has taught you to ride. I know your Papa would like that." I look back at Jack Greenwood, hoping he can see that I appreciate his relationship with my daughter. I decide to make sure he knows.

"Mr. Greenwood, thank you for being a grandfather to Charlotte. I know I haven't been here for her these first few years but I will be from now on. Your relationship with her is important to me." I pause for a moment. "I want you to know I have left my position with my father's company. It may take me a little time to find another job, but I will still be able to support Gemma and Charlotte because I have investments I can live off of until I find a new position. I have also purchased Gemma's salon. It, along with four others, is my gift to her. My father will not be able to hurt her again." I shift back and forth on my feet. Jack's silence makes me nervous.

"I am going to head back home now. Gemma wants a little time and I am going to give that to her. I want you and Mrs. Greenwood to both know that I love Gemma and Charlotte. They are my life now. Nothing else matters but them."

Jack Greenwood's expression changes to one of respect. I am relieved. He extends his hand to me first this time. I take it, intending to shake it but he uses it to pull me into a hug. I awkwardly accept the hug. My father never shows affection so this catches me off guard. Maybe this is the way families are supposed to be and mine is just dysfunctional. Just as quick as he hugged me, he pulls back.

"This little one right here and that one in the house, those girls are my family. Sounds like you are going to be part of my family now too, so you need to call me Jack." He reaches down and picks up Charlotte.

"Yes sir, Jack," I smile, leaning over to give Charlotte a hug and kiss as Jack holds her. "I have to go, Charlotte. I may not see you for a couple days, but I will call you every night."

Charlotte hugs me back. She takes her little hands and places them on my face and says, "Okay, Daddy. I love you, Daddy."

"I love you too, sweetheart. Be good for your Papa and I will see you soon."

I kiss the tip of her nose and walk out of the barn. I hope Gemma doesn't take too long to think. I need those two more than either one of them can imagine.

CHAPTER NINETEEN

GEMMA

I WATCH RAEF WALK OUT THE door and do nothing to stop him. I want to run after him, but I don't. I asked him for time and he is giving it to me.

All this time I blamed Raef and it was his father. Granted, Raef listened to his father all those years ago, but his father is obviously quite manipulative.

For the man to be so despicable as to close the salon and let Tiba and I believe Raef was behind it—even after Raef had bought the place—is just shocking. I don't understand why Raef's father wants to keep him from me so badly. Maybe he feels I am not good enough for his son.

Raef told me he wants to be with me; he wants the three of us to be a family. I don't think his father will like that and I worry about Raef not having a relationship with him. Will he regret that decision down the road? I want to believe he won't, but the fear is still there.

The door opens and Kathleen comes into the house. I don't know how long I have been sitting here. I am still at the table just as I was when Raef left. Kathleen sits across from me. Her eyes look into mine as if she is attempting to see inside my mind.

"I just saw Raef leave. He came out of the barn where Jack and Charley were working on the horses. Did you two get everything straight?" Kathleen isn't trying to be nosy, she just wants to be there for me. I know this because she has been there for me for so long now.

"Yes. No. I don't know. He told me his father is the one who sent the man to close the shop. Raef didn't have anything to do with it. In fact…" I explain how Raef bought the salons, that they're mine now whether I accept him in my life or not. I look down because I don't really know what else to say about the situation. I still can't believe that he has given me five salons.

"Oh, Gemma! That's wonderful. I just knew he didn't have anything to do with that mess yesterday. And he bought you those salons? I must say that I am a little surprised he didn't keep them in his name. He obviously loves you very much." Kathleen smiles from ear to ear. When she sees that I am not smiling, she gives me a confused look.

"It was supposed to be a wedding present to me," I tell her quietly.

"A wedding present!" Kathleen shrieks with joy. "Oh, honey! That's great! I'm so excited for you! I hope it's a very short engagement. Do you want a big wedding or a small one?" Kathleen rattles on about the wedding and I know I have to stop her.

"We didn't actually get to a proposal. I asked him for some time." Kathleen looks at me with that confused look again. I know that she is wondering why I asked him for time. To be honest, I am wondering that myself right now.

"Oh, okay. Um, can I just ask why? Did he say something to upset you?"

"No, everything he said was perfect. He was perfect. I was just so overwhelmed by it all that I couldn't think. The only thing my mind kept telling me was that this was all so fast it couldn't be true. So I just asked him for some time. I wanted to stop him as he was leaving but I couldn't bring myself to do it. I was just scared." Those last words tell the whole story. I notice I'm relentlessly twisting my hands. I am scared. Scared to believe my dreams could actually be coming true. Scared to depend on what someone tells me. Scared to give my heart completely to Raef. Just scared.

Kathleen reaches across the table and takes both of my writhing hands in hers. Having my hands in those of the woman I consider my mother is an immediate comfort.

"Sweetie, I know you're scared but that man obviously loves you. And not just you but Charley too. I watched him with her when he first arrived today. That little girl has him wrapped up already. I know you're worried this is happening too quickly but sometimes you just know when it is right. He came here for you. He wanted to make sure you knew he had nothing to do with yesterday. And he bought you a business. I really believe he is in it for the long haul. You just have to be brave and let him in."

As Kathleen finishes talking, we hear the door open. Charley runs through the door with Jack behind her. She runs across the room into the kitchen and climbs into my lap. I steal a quick kiss on her nose before she starts talking.

"My daddy came and told me bye before he left.

He said he might not see me for a while. He said I could talk to him every night on the phone. Can I call him right now, Mommy?" Charley has her little hands on my cheeks, staring straight into my eyes. The love she has for her father shines brightly in her little blue eyes.

"Let's give him just a little bit of time before you call him. Why don't you run to your room and pick out something clean to wear. You need a bath after riding today. I'll be along in a few minutes to help you." I need a few more minutes with Kathleen to make sure I am making the right decisions.

"Okay, Mommy. I'm gonna pick out something pretty to wear." Charley jumps off my lap and takes off towards her room.

"That one is just a ball of energy, isn't she?" Jack says as he chuckles. I look up at him as he stands near the table. His expression becomes solemn again. "Your young man and I had a chat before he left. You know how I have felt about him, but I have to say I think I was wrong about him. That boy loves you and he loves that little girl in there. If you love him, then put him out of his misery and go get him."

Jack turns and walks back to the front door. I stare after him in shock. Jack is a man of few words and the ones he just spoke were not ones I was expecting. He has not said much about Raef over the years, but what he has said hasn't been good. He always felt Raef wasn't doing what he should to support his child, even though I had never told him he had a child. Jack's opinion was always, "A man should just know," which I think was more of a fatherly type response than anything else. Now to hear him say that I should go after Raef confuses me even more.

"He's right, Gemma. If you love that boy, you need to go after him. Don't make him wait too long. For him to come here to find you should show what you mean to him. Most men wouldn't come to the home of your ex-husband to find you. I know that none of us look at you and Max that way, but for Raef, I am sure it was uncomfortable. But he came anyway. That says something about him. If you need time, take a little but don't take too much." Kathleen stands up from her seat. "I am going to go help Charley get a bath."

Kathleen walks away, leaving me with my thoughts. The points both Jack and Kathleen have made make sense to me. I love Raef. I never stopped loving him. He came here to tell me he loves me even though he had never met these people. It is settled. I can't let him go. I have to go to him.

With my mind made up, I am filled with a sudden excitement about getting to Raef. I jump up, practically running through the house to find Kathleen helping Charley get ready for her bath.

"Would you mind if Charley stayed here tonight?" I say before I can change my mind. Charley rarely stays anywhere without me so Kathleen looks a little shocked by my request. "I'm going to find Raef."

Smiling at that statement Kathleen looks at Charley and asks, "How bought a sleepover with us tonight? I bet we can get Papa to watch a princess movie with us?"

Charley jumps up and down while turning to me for approval. When she sees my quick nod, she turns back to Kathleen. "Yes, Mums, I want to stay!" Then she turns back to me. "You'll be okay without me won't you, Mommy?" My little girl is so sweet.

"Yes, I will. I think it will be fun for you." I pick her up to give her a hug. Hugs from Charley are the best. "I'll come back and pick you up tomorrow. You be good for Papa and Mums." I give her a kiss and another tight hug before putting her back down.

Charley goes back to choosing toys to put in the bathtub. I give Kathleen a quick hug and I whisper, "Thank you," before leaving the room. As I rush through the house, I realize I don't have a way to get back into town. I guess I should have thought of that before I made plans to go after Raef. Jack finds me standing in the living room looking lost.

"What's wrong, girlie? Did something happen?" The concern shows on his face.

"Well, everything was about to be great. I was going to go after Raef. Then I realized I don't have a vehicle." I twist my hands as I talk. Jack reaches in his pocket and pulls out a ring of keys. Without saying anything he works a key off the ring. When he is done, he holds it out to me.

"Here you go. Take Kathleen's car. If we need to go anywhere, we can take my truck." Jack places the key in my hand and closes my fingers around it.

"Jack, are you sure?"

"Of course, I am! You know we would give you anything we have, you just won't let us. Take the car and go get your young man." Jack give me a hug and turns to walk away. He stops and turns back to say, "Bring him back with you. I think I may like to get to know him."

After I get settled in the car, I pause for a moment to catch my breath. I am heading out after Raef with no plan. I just know that I have to see him now. Pulling out my cell phone, I send off a quick text to Raef.

Me: Can you meet me at my apartment in about an hour?

I start the car and head down the farm's road as I wonder how long it will take him to respond. Or even if he will respond at all. I don't have to ponder that question for long when I hear my phone notify me of a new message. I quickly look to see if it is Raef. I slow to a stop to read it.

Raef: There is nothing in this world that could keep me away. See you in an hour. I love you.

I smile and hold the phone to my heart for a moment. I am going to grab my happily ever after. Putting the phone down, I quickly start back on my journey. This next hour can't pass quickly enough.

CHAPTER TWENTY

RAEF

I SMILE. GEMMA WANTS TO SEE me. I never expected to hear from her so quickly but I am certainly glad I did. She probably thinks I am headed back to my apartment in the city but little does she know that I stopped in Granier. I just couldn't bring myself to go back to my empty apartment. Something about being here in Granier makes me feel closer to her.

Since I have an hour to spare, I decide to leave the coffee shop where I have been since getting back into town. A quick visit to the salon will pass the time and allow me to make sure nothing has happened since I was last there. With the things that have happened over the last few days, I wouldn't put anything past my father.

Pulling up to the shop, I see that the outside looks good. I let myself in with the key I kept for myself. Everything seems to be in order on the inside. I venture over to Gemma's station and sit in the chair. Her little counter looks bare without the pictures of Charlotte adorning it. The thought of her removing those pictures and all of her other things breaks my heart. That feeling only lasts for a moment. As soon as she is ready, she can bring all of her stuff back. This place is now hers.

I can't wait for Charlotte to meet my family. That is, everyone but my father. My mother is going to be so excited to do all the things a grandmother does. I am not really sure what those things are, but I know my mom will be the best at it. Not that she will be better than Kathleen has obviously been for Charlotte, but she will be equally as good. Thinking of my mom, I pull out my phone to send her a message.

Me: Hey Mom, just checking on you. I talked to Gemma. She asked for time but seems to have changed her mind. We are meeting up again in just a little while. I'll keep you posted.

Mom doesn't always keep her phone with her so I am surprised when I get a message back so quickly.

Mom: That's great! You be sure to bring Gemma and my beautiful granddaughter to see me as soon as you can. Love you, Son.

Smiling, I tuck my phone back into my pocket and let my thoughts drift to Gemma. I reach into my pocket and pull out the ring I purchased for her. All I want to do is make her my wife. I can only hope she wants to talk to me because she is ready for that step. I can't even imagine if she wants to tell me that we are over. That just can't be it. Gemma and Charlotte are my family now. We have to be because I won't accept any other option.

My watch shows me that more time has passed than I realized. It is time for me to head to Gemma's apartment. My heart is already beating faster in anticipation of seeing her and hearing what she has to say. I take one last look around the salon and then move out the door. After locking the door and walking back to my car, I am on my way to see Gemma.

The drive to her apartment is short but it is long enough for me to consider where we will live. I can't expect Gemma and Charlotte to move into the city to live in my apartment. It isn't a family apartment and definitely not what we need. I suppose we could stay in Gemma's apartment for a period of time. I would really love to purchase a house for us and that had been my plan. Now that I am unemployed I wonder if we should wait.

Remembering that I am unemployed brings other thoughts to my mind. Will Gemma think I am no good for her and Charlotte now? Will she be worried that I can't support my family? I just have to make sure she understands that I am financially stable enough to support us, all three of us, until I can find another position. With my history at the family company, I think I can find a position fairly quickly. My priority right now is making our family whole. The work can come later.

I notice the lights are on in the apartment. There is a moment of relief for me in knowing she has not changed her mind. I had not even thought about how Gemma was going to get back into town from the farm. I notice a car parked by hers that looks like one that was at the farm. She must have driven home in it.

Knowing the way things have been, I feel I need to knock and not just go in like usual. I rap on the door lightly. Almost as quickly as I knock, the door opens. I am face to face with my Gemma. She looks beautiful. My breath is taken away as I wait for her to speak. I am rewarded with a shy smile as she moves aside to allow me to enter.

"I'm glad you came." Her sweet voice covers me.

I wonder how she could ever think that I wouldn't come.

"I was thrilled to hear from you." I grab her hand as I walk by and she follows me into the living room. "Let's sit."

Gemma sits next to me on the couch, right beside me. It is then that I finally look around the room and notice that the light is coming only from a lamp and various candles that are lit and placed romantically all around the room. My heart feels lighter. This has to mean Gemma wants me as much as I want her.

"I love you, Raef," Gemma suddenly says to me. She seems embarrassed as her cheeks turn the cutest shade of pink. I release her hand only so I can place both of mine on her face. I pull her in for the lightest of kisses.

"I love you too, Gemma. I love you more than life itself." I can't help myself. I kiss her again. When I pull away from her lips our eyes connect. I can see the love shining in her eyes.

"I'm so sorry about earlier. I was just overwhelmed and scared. I don't want to be scared anymore. I never stopped loving you, Raef. I want to be with you. I want Charley to have her daddy all the time. I want what you said you want. I want us to be a family." Gemma's words wrap around me and warm me from the inside out. My heart bursts with love for my beautiful Gemma.

"Gemma, I am so glad you feel that way! I had decided that even if you told me we couldn't be together, I would never be able to let you go. Not again. My life is nothing without you. I know that now. I want you and Charlotte with me every day from this point on." I kiss her one more time before digging into my pocket. Finding what I am looking for, I move from the couch to my knee.

Gemma looks shocked, covering her mouth with one hand. I hold out the ring, take her hand in mine, and kiss the top of it.

"When I first met you I knew you were special. More than that, I knew you were mine. I loved you in a way I never imagined could happen. Stupidly I walked away from you. I tried to convince myself that I didn't love you. The minute I laid eyes on you again, I knew I had been lying to myself. I love you more than you can ever imagine. You are the light in my heart that has been missing for the last five years. I can't imagine another minute without you. You have given me the two most precious gifts I could ever receive—your love and our daughter. Gemmaline Warren, will you do me the honor of being my wife? Will you marry me so we can spend the rest of our days together?"

It may not have been the perfect setting, but my words were straight from my heart. Tears stream down Gemma's face. I suddenly realize she is nodding.

"Yes, Raef! I will marry you!" Gemma catapults herself off the couch and into my arms. I hold her as tightly as possible. She kisses me like both of our lives depend on that kiss. I feel every bit of her love. She pulls away and rests her head on my forehead. We sit like that without saying anything for quite some time. I finally move Gemma back a little and bring my hand back around to show her the ring.

"Let's make it official." I take her left hand and slowly slide the ring on her finger. I take my time and savor the moment. The ring fits perfectly. This moment makes me ready to put one more ring on that finger and make her my wife. I will give her any kind of wedding she wants, but I sure hope she doesn't want to wait too long while planning one.

"It's beautiful, Raef. It's perfect. I love it." Gemma looks away from the ring and back to me. "Are we really engaged?" Laughing at the sound of awe in her voice, I pull her back to my chest.

"Yes, sweetheart, we are really engaged, and I am never letting you go." I pull us into a standing position without letting go of Gemma. I kiss her softly but it quickly turns into a much more passionate kiss. "Do we need to pick up Charlotte or do we have a little time?"

"She's spending the night with Kathleen and Jack. I was kind of hoping we could have tonight for just us." Gemma tucks her head as she says the last part. Her shyness still takes over sometimes. That warrants another kiss.

"In that case, I would very much like to make love to my fiancé." I take her lips as I mold her to me. My hands slowly wander over her body and our tongues dance in a kiss that has me on fire. I am sure that Gemma can feel exactly what she is doing to me with our bodies pressed together. Her hands move across my chest and arms as we kiss like we haven't had each other in years instead of days. It reminds me of the first time we were together after finding each other again. The sense of urgency is overwhelming. When I can't take it anymore I pull back. We are both breathing rapidly as I take Gemma's hand and pull her toward the bedroom.

"I can't wait any longer, Gem. I want to see all of you, feel all of you and love all of you." As we enter her bedroom, I quickly divest her of her clothing. Just as quickly as I removed hers, I remove mine. I grab her and pull her back to me, feeling her skin against mine. The feeling is so superb that I hear myself moaning. I am not alone as I hear a small moan escape from Gemma also.

Slowly I back Gemma up to the bed. I lay her down, me over her without ever breaking our kiss. The feeling of being with her like this is almost too much. I don't want this to be over too quickly so I know I have to slow myself down. Moving my lips from hers, I trail kisses down the side of her neck. I continue down to her breast. I kiss all around her breast but avoid her nipple. Gemma's moans urge me on. When she least expects it, I take her nipple between my lips and gently bite it with my teeth. Not only her sounds reward me, but her hands in my hair urge me on.

As Gemma writhes under me, I move to the other breast and give it the same attention as the first. Her hands in my hair tighten. Like the whisper of a feather, my fingers glide over her skin. Finding the place I want, I feel the wetness on my fingers. She is definitely ready for me. Inserting a finger inside her, I use my thumb to caress her nub. I feel her tighten around my finger as an orgasm overtakes her.

Hearing Gemma call my name as she comes is a very heady feeling. I can't wait any longer. I position myself between her legs and kiss her hard as she rides the last bit of her orgasm. When I pull back from her lips, I see the glassy look of satisfaction in her eyes.

"Gem, no condom tonight. We are engaged and I want a house full of babies." I have my hardness in my hand and am rubbing against her.

"No condom. Just let me feel you, Raef."

I don't need to hear any more words from her. I

place myself at her entrance and slowly work my way inside. She is so tight it takes some time for me to get in but when I do it is heaven. I still for a moment. The feeling of being bare inside her is enough to push me over the edge right now. I regain control and begin to move inside her.

"You feel so good, Gem. I don't think I can make this last very long." I pick up speed as Gemma meets me thrust for thrust. I can feel the burn building and know that I am close. I reach between us to caress her bundle of nerves once again. It does the trick and in only a few moments Gemma is coming again, calling my name as she does. As her muscles contract around me, I go over the edge. With a roar, I come inside of her. It is more than a feeling of sexual release; it is a total emotional experience.

My weight suddenly seems more than I can support over Gemma, so I gently roll us on our sides without ever losing our connection. Her head lays on my arm as we both catch our breath. My hand slides up and down her back caressing her bare skin. Her small hands rest on my chest. I feel the most content in this moment than any other moment I have ever experienced. To know that I get to experience this for the rest of my life has me already hardening again.

Gemma chuckles against my chest. "I can feel you growing inside me. You didn't get enough the first time?"

Groaning, I pull her even tighter to me. "I can't help it. You do that to me. It feels so good to know that I get to do this with you for the rest of my life. It made me want you all over again." I begin to move inside her. Just small movements, but enough to make her squirm against me.

Rolling onto my back, I pull Gemma on top of me. She sits up and I take in the view that is all Gemma. The sight of her is so beautiful it almost brings tears to my eyes. As she begins to move above me, I let her take complete control. My hands wander along her body and I wonder how I got so fortunate to have this second chance with her.

CHAPTER TWENTY-ONE

GEMMA

THE SOUND OF KATHLEEN'S RINGTONE on my phone awakens me. Raef's body is wrapped around mine and he appears to still be asleep. We obviously dozed off. I slowly ease my way out of his arms and reach for my phone. If it had been anyone other than Kathleen, I would have ignored it. I step out of my bedroom as I answer. Before I can say hello, I hear Kathleen calling my name.

"Gemma! Gemma! She is gone! Charley is gone!" Kathleen's distraught voice screams into the phone. Panic seizes me. What does she mean *Charley is gone*?

"What do you mean?" I can barely speak to get the words out.

"He took her! Jack and Charley were in the barn feeding the horses when he came in. He started out just talking to Jack but when Jack turned his back to him, he hit him in the head and knocked him out. He took Charley!" Kathleen's words come out quickly and the despair is evident. None of it makes sense to me. Fear is the only thing I feel.

"Who, Kathleen? Who took her?" I re-enter the bedroom to wake Raef.

"Charles Alvero took her. Raef's father."

Panic courses through my veins. My knees weaken and I have to grab the doorknob to keep myself from sinking to the floor. I can hear the sound of Kathleen crying and Jack's booming voice in the background. Raef is no longer asleep. He is staring at his own phone. His eyes lift to meet mine.

"He has her, Gemma. My *father* has our baby." Raef says the word *father* with nothing but contempt. He crosses the room and pulls me into his arms as I sob against him. I hand him my phone because I can no longer speak.

"Hello?" Raef says through his own tears.

"Raef? Oh my God, Raef. I am so sorry! Your father knocked Jack in the head and took her! We've got to find her! What do we do?" I can hear Kathleen even though Raef has the phone.

"How long has he been gone? Have you called the police?" I quickly begin to get dressed while Raef talks. The quicker we can get out of here the quicker we can find her. Raef nods at whatever Kathleen is saying and quickly ends the call. As he hands me my phone, he pulls me back into his arms.

"It is going to be okay, Gem. My father may be crazy but he isn't going to hurt her. He is trying to get to me. Jack has already talked to the Sheriff's Department and they are on their way to the farm. Max is on his way there also. We will be there soon." Raef places a quick kiss on top of my head and lets me go. I see the tears still on his face. He is just as affected by this as I am.

I finish dressing as Raef throws on his clothes. Before we leave the apartment, Raef tries to call his father. When there is no answer, he texts him. Maybe he will just meet us and give Charley to us. Raef's phone dings with a message.

"What does it say?" I ask Raef before he has time to read the message. Once he has read it, he looks away from the phone.

"He said the only way we get Charlotte is for me to meet him tomorrow and withdraw my resignation." Raef's voice is laced with anger. "He said he will give Charlotte to you once I do, but only if I agree to walk away from both of you."

I don't know what to think. I can't wait until tomorrow to get her from Charles Alvero. We have to do something now.

"We can't wait until tomorrow, Raef. We just can't."

"We aren't waiting. We'll find him and get Charlotte back. He thinks this is a game." Raef places his hand on my back and gently pushes me toward the door. "I'm not going to let him play games with our daughter."

We lock the apartment and run to Raef's car. We are quickly on the road to the farm. Raef is driving at a high rate of speed and I don't complain. While he drives, Raef makes a call from his car. I see the name Daniel on the screen. He must be calling his brother.

Daniel answers after only one ring. "You must be in some kind of trouble to call me at this time of night." Glancing at the car clock I see it is almost 10:00 P.M.

"Not me, Daniel. Charlotte. Dad kidnapped Charlotte from the Greenwood's farm. I need you to go to Mom's and the two of you call all of his friends. We need to figure out where he may have taken her." Raef's hands tighten on the steering wheel as he speaks. His knuckles are white from gripping it so tightly.

"Shit!" Daniel shouts through the phone. I hear rustling in the background and the jingle of keys. "I am headed that way right now. Call Mom and tell her I am on my way. I knew that fucker was crazy but I had no idea he would do something like this." The sound of a door slamming and running footsteps comes through the speakers of the car.

"I didn't either, Daniel. We just have to find him quickly. Gemma is going to text you the address to the farm in case you and Mom need it." Raef tosses me his phone. I quickly open messages and find Daniel's name. I shoot a quick message with Jack & Kathleen's address. Daniel's voice comes back through the speakers along with the sound of his car starting.

"Got the address. Call Mom. I'm headed to her house right now. And little brother, it's going to be okay. We will find Charlotte. I love you, man. I'll see you as quickly as I can get there." Daniel ends the connection.

Raef quickly hits another button on the screen and the word Mom pops up. After just a couple of rings, his mother picks up.

"Well hello, Son. I wasn't expecting to hear from you this late. Is everything okay?" The worry in her voice is evident. I feel certain that casual conversation at this time of night is not the norm for Raef and his mother.

"Mom, Dad has taken Charlotte. He knocked Jack in the head and took her. We are headed there now. Daniel is on his way to your house. I need you to call all of Dad's friends and see if anyone might know where he is." The gasp from Raef's mother echoes through the car as he tells her what has happened.

"Oh, Raef. Why would Charles do something like

this?" Sobbing follows. As with Daniel, I can hear rustling in the background. Doors opening, hangers rattling, doors closing. All sounds of her getting dressed.

"He's trying to control me, Mom. I've never gone against him before. He's obviously more unstable than any of us thought. He sent me a single text message that said, 'I have your precious daughter. Maybe now you will do what I tell you to do.' That was all he said." Until this point I hadn't even thought about the fact that Raef knew Charley was gone when I walked back into the room. My mind so shocked by what Kathleen was telling me that I didn't even question that he knew. "He wouldn't answer my call, but when I texted him back, he basically said he will give Charlotte to Gemma as long as I agree to his demands. It's a power play but we have to get to them as quickly as we can. I have no idea what he has going on in his crazy mind right now. I can't risk him hurting Charlotte."

"We'll find them, Raef. I should have seen the signs and been able to stop this." Ruth sobs through the phone, "I'm so sorry!"

"It isn't your fault, Mom. Just Dad's."

Even with the ice cold fear flowing through me, it warms my heart to know that this woman who has never met Charley seems to be as distraught as we are. She will be a wonderful grandmother to Charley one day. I just hope we find our daughter in time for that to happen. That thought brings even more tears and a sob catches in my throat.

Raef ends the call with his mother. Her voice seemed to calm him and he relaxes his hold on the steering wheel slightly. I stare out the window and watch as the scenery passes quickly due to our speed.

"Hey," Raef says softly as he takes my hand in his. His eyes glance over to mine before turning back to the road. "We're going to find her. My father may be crazy but I hope he is smart enough not to hurt Charlotte." I nod even though I know Raef can't see it with his eyes on the road.

Raef's grip on my hand tightens. As the car slows, I realize we are turning into the farm road. The trip out here only took about half of the normal time. Raef must have driven faster than I realized. He speeds down the gravel road toward the house. From the distance I can see multiple vehicles parked at the house. As we get closer, I see that there are four Sheriff's department cars along with Max's truck. Raef quickly parks the car and we exit. The door to the house opens suddenly and Kathleen runs towards the car.

My speed picks up. She meets me with her arms open and tears flowing down her cheeks. Her tight grip around me makes me feel somewhat calmer.

"We are so sorry for letting this happen, Gemma!" Kathleen cries as she holds me. "We love Charley so much. We should have protected her better." Raef catches up by this point with Jack reaching us from the other direction.

Raef puts his arm around Kathleen even as she holds me. "This isn't your fault. This is all my father. Please don't blame yourself. Gemma and I know how much you love Charlotte." Kathleen releases me just long enough to hug Raef before putting her arm back around me.

As Kathleen turns to lead me toward the house, I see Jack extend his hand to Raef. Raef takes his hand but pulls him into a hug. I hear Raef speaking quietly to Jack but I can't make out the words. Finally, Jack nods as Raef ends the hug and they follow behind us into the house.

Several uniformed officers wait inside the house. I recognize the Sheriff and a few of the deputies that I know. They each come over to hug me and reassure me that they will find Charley. I can't seem to find my voice to speak to any of them.

The Sheriff tells us they have reason to believe Charlotte may be being held somewhere close to the farm. There is only one road into this area and a deputy has been parked on it all night monitoring speeds. Jack described the vehicle to the deputy who remembers seeing it come into the area but never seeing it leave. There are multiple camping areas past the farm and they are currently working on the best way to search the area.

When the Sheriff points toward the kitchen, I see it has been turned into a makeshift office with a large map laid out on the table. I see Max bent over the map. He seems to be studying it intently, his finger moving across it.

"Max," I sob as I enter the kitchen. He turns when he hears my voice. His eyes mist over and he moves to take me into his arms. I cry into his chest as he tries to comfort me.

"Shhh, Gemma. Don't cry so hard. It's going to be okay. We're going to find Charley. You need to be calm so you can help us. You'll make yourself sick like this." His hand strokes my hair. His voice is softer than normal and calms me. His friendship at this particular moment means so much to me. I nod into his chest and attempt to curtail my sobs. After a few minutes

I realize I am much calmer and pull back from Max.

"Thank you Max. You always know how to calm me down. I am scared to death right now but you are right. I am no good to Charley if I am a sobbing, blubbering mess." I notice a movement out of the corner of my eye and see Raef watching us. There is immense sadness in his eyes. He has made no move to interfere with Max's effort to calm me. His normal jealous eyes are not showing. The blue of his eyes shine brightly with tears for our daughter.

I look quickly back to Max. He watches me while glancing at Raef. Max pulls me back into a quick hug and whispers in my ear, "Go to him, Gemma. He needs you right now." Max releases me and turns back to the table that is now surrounded by Jack, Kathleen and several of the officers. I watch for a brief moment as all of these people converse over the map.

Turning back to Raef, I walk slowly over to him. He doesn't move but watches me as I approach. A lone tear trails down his cheek as I reach him. We stand for a moment with inches between us as we stare into each other's eyes. I reach for him and he quickly grabs me, pulling me tightly into him. I feel the wetness of his tear against my cheek. We don't speak any words, we just hold each other.

CHAPTER TWENTY-TWO

RAEF

MY PHONE DINGS WITH A message from Daniel. He and Mom have had no luck with any of Dad's friends. There is one more person they haven't been able to reach, so they aren't giving up yet. Frustrated with the progress, I walk into the kitchen.

I watch as Max comforts Gemma. The old feeling of jealously is there but the fear for Charlotte keeps it at bay. I feel helpless. Helpless to find Charlotte. Helpless to comfort Gemma. In this moment, I feel totally alone in the world. Deep inside I know this is a ridiculous feeling but that doesn't help me push it down. I lean against the kitchen counter watching Gemma and Max.

Officers enter the kitchen and I see them surround the map on the table. Jack and Kathleen follow behind them. I can't tear my eyes from Gemma and Max. I love her so damn much but my attempts to comfort her pale in comparison to Max. I feel tears in my eyes. Tears for my daughter. Tears for Gemma. I have the momentary thought that this may be the thing that takes her away from me. My father may succeed in taking my daughter and my fiancé in one night.

Gemma turns to me and her eyes meet mine. I wish I could read what was going on in her head right now. Tear stains cover her beautiful face. Her brown eyes are large and dark, fear evident. After a few moments, she turns away from me and back to Max. I feel like a knife is going through my heart as he hugs her again. I see him whispering in her ear. His hug is quick. After, he turns back to the table and jumps into the discussion with the officers. Gemma watches him for a few moments before turning back to me.

I don't move. The next move has to be hers. My father has taken our daughter. I know that there must be a part of Gemma that blames me for all of this right now. If I am going to be there for her, then I have to make sure I let her choose to come to me. We need to be on the same page to do the best for finding our daughter. Gemma stares at me for a few moments before slowly moving my direction. I stand perfectly still. She stops in front of me, close enough I can almost feel her breath. I feel every nerve in my body at this moment. The tear that escaped my eye as she approached now feels like a weight upon my cheek.

When Gemma moves her hands toward me I can take it no longer. I quickly pull her against me, wrapping my arms around her so tightly I'm afraid she can't breathe. I loosen my grip slightly but still hold on tightly. Neither of us say anything, we just stand there holding each other. There is conversation all around us, but my brain can't put it all together.

We stand holding each other for quite some time. I know that I need to be involved with the discussion happening with the officers from the Sheriff's Department but I can't pull myself away from Gemma. We both seem to need the comfort from each other. I don't know how much time has passed when I pull back.

"Gem, I need to see what is happening. I need to know if they have any progress on where to look for Charlotte." Gemma nods but doesn't speak. I kiss her on the forehead and walk to the table where everyone has gathered. It seems everyone is talking at the same time and I can't distinguish anything from the conversation.

Hearing the front door open, I look up and see an officer walk in with my mother. Daniel walks in behind them with his phone to his ear. I turn Gemma to where she can see them. They are all walking quickly toward the kitchen. Mom is quietly talking with the officer as they reach the others. Daniel, still on the phone, speaks as they enter the room.

"I think we know where they are." Daniel's words grab the attention of everyone in the room and all eyes turn to him. Gemma and I move apart from each other. Grabbing her hand, I move closer to Daniel.

"Where are they?" I ask Daniel anxiously.

"I have his friend Carl Dubeaux on the phone. Dad called him yesterday wanting to use his camp for a few days. Carl thought he just wanted to get away for a bit so he gave him the key and told him to stay as long as he wants." Daniel looks around the room. "He wants to speak to the Sheriff."

Sheriff Jones walks to where Daniel is holding the phone. "Sheriff Des Jones." He takes the phone from Daniel and begins to speak to the person on the other end. Daniel turns to me.

"I knew Dad had to have somewhere to go." Daniel's excitement is apparent. "And I knew it would be somewhere we wouldn't know about. Carl is his closest friend so I hoped he would know something about where Dad might be. It just took us awhile to get in touch with him. I never expected for him to know exactly where he is."

Mom walks over and hugs me and then Gemma. "It is almost over, Son. We know where they are. Now we just have to go get them."

"Thank you, Daniel," I say as I move toward the door. "I would have never thought about calling Carl. Let's go get Charlotte,"

"Wait a minute." The Sheriff's words stop me. "We have to do this the right way. We don't want him to slip away or do something to the child. Let's get a plan together before anyone runs in half-cocked." The Sheriff is right. I can't risk him hurting Charlotte.

"I have the location of the camp. Let's get back to the map and figure out the best way to handle this," the Sheriff says as he moves back to the kitchen. His men follow him back to the table.

Gemma stands alone in the middle of the room. My mom seems to notice her at the same time I do. She rushes over to give her a hug.

"It's going to be okay. We know where your baby is now. We're going to get her back." Mom keeps her arm around Gemma and turns back to me. She gives me a smile and a nod to let me know she will stay with Gemma. I nod back and head back to the room with the officers.

After what I consider a long discussion, the Sheriff and I decide that I need to be the one to approach the camp. Officers will be in place around the building to cover me. I will be outfitted with a body mic that will allow the Sheriff to hear what is happening. Once inside, my goal will be to get to Charlotte. I need to either get her out of the building or have both of us secured inside a room away from my father. I will also wear a bullet proof vest. We don't feel my father has any weapons since he has never owned any, but we'll be cautious.

The vehicles will park down the road from Carl's camp. From that point, the officers will all move into their positions on foot. Once placed, the Sheriff will be notified and I will drive my car on to the camp. The Sheriff will follow but will stop before getting too close to the camp. He will remain there with Gemma and Mom. Daniel and the Greenwoods will stay behind at the vehicle location with one of the officers.

After going over the plan another time, the Sheriff feels we are ready to move. The whole group heads for Carl's camp. The camp is actually fairly close to the Greenwood's farm so the drive should be short. I am really happy about that fact so I can get to Charlotte sooner rather than later.

Two of the officers stay behind at the farm just in case my father shows up there. Quite the parade of vehicles travel with the Sheriff's SUV leading the way. Gemma and I are in my car right behind the Sheriff. Daniel and Mom are in his car and Jack, Kathleen and Max are in Max's truck. The deputies are all behind everyone else.

We all meet up and take over the yard of a camp a few miles from Carl's camp. The Sheriff knows the owner. After quickly parking, we all introduce ourselves to the police officers that have met us there. I am outfitted with a bullet-proof vest and body mic system under my shirt. While this is happening, the Sheriff goes over the plan with me one more time.

After they are sure I am ready, the officers assigned to the camp where my father and Charlotte are located leave on foot. While we wait for them to notify the Sheriff that they are in position, I pull Gemma aside. I need to talk to her one more time before I do this.

"Gemma. I promise I'm going to do everything in my power to make sure Charlotte doesn't get hurt. Please have faith in me. I need to know you are with me on this." I stare into her eyes imploring her to believe in me. When she speaks it is so soft I barely hear her.

"I know you will, Raef. Just be careful in there. Come back to me with our daughter." Gemma leans into my arms. I pull away when I hear the Sheriff call my name.

"I love you, Gemma. I love you with my whole heart." I kiss Gemma then turn to head to my vehicle.

"I love you too, Raef! Please be careful!" I give her a quick look over my shoulder and a thumbs-up.

"Everyone is in place." The Sheriff has a look of concern on his face. "Are you ready for this, Raef?"

"I'm ready. Let's go get my daughter." I give him one final nod and get in my car. I see Gemma and my mother get into his SUV. Daniel and the others wave to us as we pull onto the road.

As much as I want to speed on to Carl's camp, I drive reasonably. I don't want to attract any attention from my father. I hope he is asleep and doesn't hear me until I knock on the door. The element of surprise should work in my favor. I have never been to Carl's camp so I slow down to make sure I turn into the correct drive. The last thing I need is to go banging on the wrong door.

Just after seeing the Sheriff stop his car and let me go alone, I see the number of the camp shining in my headlights and slowly turn into the drive. I can vaguely see his parking lights in the distance as a reminder that he is not far away.

After turning into the drive, I immediately see my father's car parked by the front steps. I ease my car behind his, pulling to a stop at his back bumper. There is no way he can get his car out of the drive with me parked like this. If he tries to run, it will have to be on foot. Before I get out, I take a look at the camp. It has an expansive front porch but no porch light lit. Lights shine through the windows though, so my father may be awake. I exit my car, quietly close my door and tuck the key in my pocket so he can't escape in my car.

There are no signs he has heard anything so I walk up the steps to the porch. A board squeaks under my feet as I cross from the steps to the door. My heart jumps, but I don't hear any movement from inside. It appears I have made it this far undetected. I open the screen door as quietly as possible. I take one last deep breath to calm my nerves and then knock loudly on the front door.

"Let me in, Dad. It's me, Raef." As much as I don't want to call him Dad or act like I am being nice, I know that I have to for Charlotte's safety. I rap on the door again. "Come on Dad! Answer the door."

I hear heavy footsteps from inside. I steel myself as my father jerks the door open. I am suddenly face to face with my father's sneer.

"Well, what do we have here in the middle of the night? When you didn't return my text I assumed you were waiting until we could meet tomorrow. I guess I was wrong." My father spits out his words with the sneer never leaving his face.

"Can I come in? I want to see Charlotte." I'm already pushing my way inside the door. My father steps back.

"Of course you can come in. That kid of yours is asleep, though. Cute kid. Reminds me of Marie when she was little. She didn't even have a clue that I took her. She thinks she is camping with her 'pappy.' That's what she started calling me." There is disgust in his voice as he says those last words.

I survey the room. He isn't holding any type of weapon and I don't see anything visible in the room that looks like a weapon. That is good news. Now I just need to get to Charlotte.

"Where is she? I'll just peak in on her while she sleeps. You won't keep me from that, will you?" I look at my father for his reaction to my question. He flinches slightly but quickly hides it.

"She is in one of the bedrooms. I will tell you which one after you tell me how you found us." Charles Alvero is a stubborn man. He took Charlotte for a reason and I know he won't let me see her until he gets his point across. He stands before me with his arms crossed as if he has drawn a line in the sand.

"Daniel thought to call Carl. You didn't bother to tell Carl you were planning to kidnap your grand-daughter when you asked for his camp, did you?" I can't help but bite out those words.

"I didn't kidnap her. I just borrowed her for a little while. I needed something to get you to talk to me. Looks like it worked. Now you just have to agree to come back to work and leave that little whore of yours and all this will be behind us." He still thinks he can manipulate me into being his minion again. He has obviously gone so far off his rocker that he doesn't even realize what he has done.

"Gemma is not a whore and I will not go back to work with you." I know I am poking the bear when I should be agreeing with him but I just can't help it. I can't bring myself to say the words he wants to hear. I walk backwards to the hall where I assume I will find the bedrooms. I don't take my eyes off of my father.

"Come on now, Son. I won't even argue with you over the kid anymore. She's damn cute. I just won't have you tied up with her mother. I'll even help you fight for the kid. That's a compromise, isn't it? You keep the kid and drop the woman. You come back and take your rightful place in the company and all will be fine." He takes a few steps toward me but lets me continue down the hall. I decide not to respond to him, keeping my full focus on finding which room holds my daughter.

The door to the first room is open. The bed is a mess and a suitcase sits on a chair. This must be the room my father was using. I continue on to the next door. This one is on the opposite side of the hall. It is open, just a bathroom. I look back. My father has closed the front door and moved toward the hall. He steadily heads toward me. I know I need to hurry before he has the chance to get to the room that holds Charlotte. I move more quickly down the hall to the last door. This has to be the one. It is partially shut so I push it open. There in the bed lies my beautiful daughter, sound asleep, oblivious to what is happening around her.

I quickly enter the room, closing and locking the

door behind me. I speak clearly so that the Sheriff can hear me through the body mic. "I have Charlotte secured in a bedroom. I saw no weapons." I move to the bed and pull Charlotte into my lap and my arms.

"Hey, beautiful girl. Wake up for me." I kiss her cheeks and she rouses from her sleep.

"Hey, Daddy," she says drowsily. "What are you doing here?"

"I couldn't stay away from my little princess so I came to find you." As I speak I hear the commotion in the front of the camp. It's obvious that the officers have entered the camp and are taking my father into custody. Charlotte notices the noise even though I try to keep her from it. She sits up in my lap.

"What's that, Daddy? What's happening?" Charlotte asks with fear in her voice.

"It's okay, princess. It's just some friends of mine that came to take my father somewhere. You know who my father is. The man who brought you here." I rub her little back trying to calm her.

"Yeah, Daddy. I know him. I fell asleep and woke up here with him. I didn't want to stay, but he let me watch TV and told me if I was a good girl we could call you and Mommy tomorrow." Charlotte seems calmer and relaxes in my lap. "Did your friends come to get him because he brought me here?"

My child is too smart for her age. I just hope this doesn't hurt her emotionally. The thought of her having problems from this makes me feel sick. Gemma and I will just have to make sure that Charlotte has the resources she needs to deal with what has happened.

"Yes. He didn't have permission to bring you here so they came with me to get him. It is quiet out there now so why don't we go out front. Your mommy is here and I know she wants to see you too." I stand up, still holding Charlotte in my arms and begin to walk out of the room.

As we enter the living room, the front door opens, and Gemma runs in. Not far behind her is my mom. Charlotte turns her little head from my chest as Gemma runs toward her.

"Mommy!" she says as I set her to the ground. Charlotte runs to meet Gemma in the living room. Gemma lifts her into her arms and just holds her.

"Hey, my little one. Are you okay? I have missed you so much!" Gemma looks over Charley's little body looking for any signs of injury.

"I'm good, Mommy. I woke up here with Pappy. He said I could call you tomorrow." Gemma looks up from Charlotte to me. "Daddy said that Pappy didn't have per…per…what was that word Daddy?" Charlotte looks at me inquiringly.

"Permission, princess. Your Pappy didn't have permission to bring you here." I smile at Gemma and move forward to wrap my arms around both of them. "But you are back with us now and no one is ever going to take you somewhere without permission again." I kiss Charlotte on the top of the head and see my mother standing awkwardly on the other side of the room.

"Charlotte, would you like to meet my mom? She is here to check on you too." I tilt my head toward where my mother is standing. Charlotte wiggles to get out of Gemma's arms and quickly runs over to my mother.

"Hi! I'm Charlotte Rae Warren. Well, now I'm Charlotte Rae Warren Alvero 'cause I have my daddy's name now too. Are you my grandma?" I chuckle at how forward my daughter is. I can't hide my huge smile at the fact that she remembered that she now has my name.

"Hello there, Charlotte. I love your name. And yes, I am your grandma. I am so happy to finally meet you. Can I give you a hug?" My mom drops to a knee so she is eye level with Charlotte. She holds her arms open to Charlotte and suddenly I witness my mother hug her granddaughter for the first time. The tears of joy in my mother's eyes reflect my own.

Glancing over at Gemma, I see her smile while her eyes are shiny with tears. She is smiling when she looks toward me. I can't help myself and lean over to give her a quick kiss.

"Can I call you Nana?" Charlotte asks. "I don't have a Nana. I have a Mums. My other grandma died and I don't know her. I call her MiMi when I talk about her though." Did I mention that my daughter is too smart for her age?

"Of course! I will be proud to be your Nana. I can't wait to get to know you." Mom stands and takes Charlotte's hand in hers. Looking at me she says, "I think there are a few other people ready to see this little one. Do you two mind if I take her outside? The Sheriff called and told the Greenwoods and Daniel that they could come on down here. They should be outside by now."

I look at Gemma before I answer. She gives me a quick nod to let me know she is fine with the idea. "Sure Mom. I would imagine Charlotte would like to see her Mums and Papa and her Uncle Max."

The Sheriff opens the door and holds it while Mom and Charlotte walk outside. He walks in to speak to us. "Are you two okay?" he asks as he walks into the room.

We both smile. "We are better than okay now that we have our daughter back." I put my arm around Gemma as she nods in agreement.

"Your father didn't put up much of a fight when we took him into custody. We haven't found any weapons outside. We are going to process the inside now that you have had a few moments with your daughter. We did find chloroform in his car. We think he may have used it on your daughter."

"That makes sense." I look at Gemma as I speak because I haven't even had time to tell her what Charlotte had told me when I found her. "Charlotte said she fell asleep and woke up here. She also hasn't mentioned anything about seeing my father hurt Jack. He must have chloroformed her before he hit Jack."

"We have an ambulance outside. We had called one earlier when we weren't sure how all of this might go down. You should probably let them check out your daughter just to make sure she is okay, especially since there is a chance he did use the chloroform on her." I hadn't even thought of that. I was so happy to get Charlotte away from my father. The Sheriff is right, though. We do need to get Charlotte medical care.

"Thank you so much, Sheriff, for everything. We will go right now and let the EMTs check on Charlotte." I shake the hand of the man who helped us save our daughter. Gemma gives him a quick hug and thanks him.

When we walk outside, Jack is holding Charlotte. My mom and Daniel are in a conversation with Jack, Kathleen and Max. As we walk toward them, a deputy stops me and reminds me that I still have the com and vest on. I motion for Gemma to continue without me and stay behind with the deputy. While removing the items for the deputy, I watch Gemma and Jack walk to the ambulance with Jack still carrying Charlotte. Jack Greenwood is a good man. He is the type of man I thought my father was. I was wrong. My father will never be that kind of man. I just hope that I can be more like Jack and less like my father. I will make it my life's work to ensure that for Gemma and Charlotte.

CHAPTER TWENTY-THREE

GEMMA

Three Weeks Later

MY PHONE DINGS WITH A message from Raef. There are moments that I still cannot believe he is back in my life. I glance at the ring on my left hand. It still gives me butterflies every time I see it.

Raef: Hey Babe! How's Charlotte? Is therapy over yet?

For the last three weeks we have had Charley visiting a psychologist that specializes in children and families. We felt it would be the best thing for her considering what happened with Raef's father. She doesn't seem to have any long lasting problems from it, but Raef and I both felt it would be better to be proactive in the situation rather than wait for something to come up down the road. We have also done family therapy. I think it has helped us as much as it has Charley

Me: Not yet. They're running a little behind today. I'll call as soon as she is out.

As soon as I hit send, the door from the back opens. The office assistant sees me and asks me to step to the back with her as we do at the end of each visit.

"Good morning, Miss Warren. Have a seat," the

psychologist says as she motions to the couch. I sit down beside Charley and she moves over to my lap. "We have some very good news for you today," the psychologist continues.

"Great. I always like good news." I smile down at Charley.

"Charley has done very well in our sessions. I also feel that you and Raef have made outstanding strides in your relationship in this short period of time. Based on how well you are all doing and how Charley feels about your family dynamic, I think it is time to end your therapy sessions." I feel a weight lifted off my chest. This means that my daughter is going to be okay.

"That is great news! You really think Charley doesn't need to visit any longer?" I want to confirm that I heard correctly.

"That is my professional opinion. She doesn't seem to have any adverse memories of the incident. She is a completely content child, very happy to have her father in her life. The three of you have good communication. It is amazing how comfortable you are with each other. Though I honestly think you would be a family at this point without my help, I am glad to have had the opportunity to work with you. Charley is an amazingly resilient child and I feel like she is going to be just fine. Of course, if anything comes up in the future you are welcome to come back." I see nothing but assurance in the psychologist's expression.

"Thank you so much! I am very happy to hear this and I know Raef will be also. We do feel like a family now and are all excited to see what our future holds." Standing, I extend my hand.

"My pleasure. I hope to see you and your family again soon, just not in therapy." She laughs as she shakes my hand.

Charley and I say our goodbyes to the office staff on our way out. We decide to see if Raef can go to lunch with us.

After Charles Alvero's arrest, Raef's uncle begged him to come back to the company. After a few days of meetings with his uncle and his brother, he agreed to return. Part of the agreement hinged on Dexter and Daniel obtaining Charles Alvero's resignation as company president. They were successful and also were able to get him to sign over all of his ownership in the company to his wife. Now Alvero & Alvero is owned solely by Dexter Alvero and Ruth Alvero. The last few weeks have been a trying time for Raef, but things are slowly getting back to normal.

I have spent the last few weeks trying to find my happy place with work. Raef has helped me get our little company off the ground with the five salons. Even with the extensive work he has faced at Alvero, he has spent time with me visiting each salon. We have completed our business plan and all of our state business filings creating Charley's Cuts & Style. Even though I am listed as owner of the company, all profits will go into the trust that Raef had previously arranged for Charley. I was happy to place Tiba in the management position of our salon. I will continue to work part-time with her just because I like the interaction with the clients. The other part of my time will be spent with Charley.

I press the button on the dash of my new vehicle to call Raef. I am still having to adjust to all of the fancy technology in this vehicle. I was against the idea Raef buying me a new vehicle, but I have to admit that I am really enjoying it. The ringing of Raef's phone comes through the speakers.

"Hey Gem! I take it you two are done with therapy." Raef's voice comes through the speakers. It still melts my heart when I hear his voice. I wonder if that will ever change. Somehow I doubt it will.

"We are finished. And not just finished today. We have been officially kicked out of therapy." I laugh as I tell him the news.

"That's great, babe! Was the doc sure we're ready for that?" Raef questions. He is like me in that he wants to make certain Charley has no future problems from his father's actions. I quickly give him the rundown on what I was told by the psychologist.

"So, since we want to celebrate, Charley and I were wondering if you had time to do lunch with us. Somebody wants pizza," I say as Charley chips in from the back seat.

"Hey, Daddy! I want pizza with you!" Raef's chuckle comes through the speakers. I smile as I picture what his expression must look like at this moment. He sure does love that little girl.

"Well, that sounds like an invitation I can't refuse. Why don't you two swing by the office and pick me up? I'll be waiting downstairs for you." I hear rustling in the background indicating that Raef is on the move.

The drive to the office doesn't take long. Raef jumps in and we head to our favorite pizza joint. We order as soon as we arrive. We are frequent visitors so we don't need a menu.

Raef reaches across the table and takes my hand in his. I look over to see him intently staring at me.

I squirm in my seat. He looks at me like he could devour me. I feel that look throughout my body.

"Hey," I say to Raef.

"Hey," is his response. I smile at him with a smile that carries all of my feelings towards him. He gives me one of his sexy smiles in return.

"So, what is the intense look for?" I ask him as he rubs his thumb across my hand. That motion sends shivers through my body.

"Just looking at my soon-to-be wife and wondering when we are going to have this wedding." We had put off wedding plans during the family therapy with Charley. The psychologist had agreed with us even though she felt that Charley was ready for us to make that step. I was nervous to begin plans at first because I still couldn't put my full trust in Raef. Now I can and I am ready. I just haven't told him that.

"Well," I watch his expression. His smile wavers a little. "I was thinking we should start planning today."

His expression is priceless. His eyes register while his mouth hangs open. He just sits there in a stupor. I smile knowing he did not expect those words.

"Yes, yes. Let's plan this thing," he says as he shakes his head in disbelief. "Can we just skip the planning and go to the courthouse?"

Laughing, I respond, "Um, no. You know I don't want a big wedding, but I do want a nice ceremony with our family and close friends. But, we can plan it for some time soon. I don't want to wait any longer than we have to."

Raef smiles from ear to ear. He moves around the table to sit beside me. He is suddenly kissing me and hugging me at the same time we are giggling like teenagers. The commotion gets the attention of our daughter who makes her typical reaction to us kissing.

"Ugh, gross!" our four-year old says. Sometimes she sounds more like a teenager than a preschooler. We both laugh as we pull away from each other.

"Sorry, princess. I can't help it. I just love your mommy so much and can't wait for her to be my wife. Are you ready to help us plan a wedding?"

"A wedding! Yes, Daddy! Let's plan a wedding!" Charley practically yells across the restaurant.

Raef and I both laugh at her obvious excitement. He looks at me and I see nothing but love in his eyes. Love for me and love for our daughter. He tightens his arm around me as he turns back to talk to Charley about dresses. Yes, dresses. I sit smiling at the two of them just watching their interaction.

Mom and Dad, I found my happily ever after. I just wish you were here to see it. In this moment, it is almost as if I can feel their presence. They would be happy for me. This thought gives me comfort and I jump into the conversation about dresses. I smile as our pizza arrives. Today we are taking the first step toward our new beginning. This time around we are a family.

THE END

PLAYLIST

"Sirens"
Pearl Jam

"The World I Know"
Collective Soul

"Alibi"
Thirty Seconds to Mars

"House of Pain"
Faster Pussycat

"Far Away"
Nickelback

"No Good in Goodbye"
The Script

"Torn to Pieces"
Pop Evil

"Broken"
Lifehouse

"Try Sleeping with a Broken Heart"
Alicia Keys

"Selfless"
It's Alive

"December"
Collective Soul

"Bleed Out"
Blue October

"Somewhere Out There"
Our Lady Peace

"Goodbye"
Secondhand Serenade

"I'll Be"
Edwin McCain

"Endlessly"
Uncle Kracker

"How Could I?"
Oleander

"How You Learn to Live Alone"
Nashville Cast

"Letting Go"
Hinder

"Stigmatized"
The Calling

ACKNOWLEDGEMENTS

FIRST AND FOREMOST, I WANT to thank my husband for supporting me in my dream of writing. This is something I have wanted to do since I was a child. With my husband's encouragement, I am finally making my dream come true. His constant support and patience through the writing of this book has kept me on track.

In writing the kidnapping portion of the story, I realized I needed advice from a professional in the law enforcement field. Catahoula Parish Sheriff Toney Edwards came to my rescue. Together we worked through the entire process of getting Charley back to her parents. His help was invaluable and I couldn't have written that section believably without him. Thanks, Sheriff, for jumping in to help me.

Since prior to beginning this book, I have been a member of a self-publishing group hosted by Author Marie Force. More recently, I have joined an additional author group she hosts. These two groups have been such an influence on me. Not only have they provided useful information for the self-publishing aspect of writing, they have given me the encouragement to continue this process. On those days where I felt like giving up, I would read posts in these groups that showed me I am not alone. The feelings I would be fighting are the same feelings many successful authors experience. I am not sure I would have ever reached a point of completion without these groups. I certainly would have no idea where to go or what to do after writing 'The End.' Thanks Marie Force for all you do to support other authors.

I am an avid reader and have met many of my favorite authors at various signings. Since beginning this writing process, I have been amazed at the support these authors are willing to provide. Authors are a special group of people and most are more than willing to offer their help and support to others. I have been fortunate to have some of these incredible ladies offer me their support. I want to especially thank one of these ladies for her support, M.J. Fields. Thank you M.J. for messaging me and offering your support. I appreciate it more than you will ever know.

A special thanks to The Killion Group for working so patiently with me. As a brand new author, I needed guidance on everything. They made a cover that was more than I imagined it could be. The editing they provided has already made me a better author and definitely made this a better book. The best part is the patience they have shown me as I learn to navigate the waters of self-publishing.

Last but certainly not least, thanks to you, my readers. You took a chance on a new author when you purchased this book. Thank you for that. As a reader, I know how hard it can be to try a new author. You have no idea how much I appreciate you giving my first book a chance.

I hope you enjoyed Raef and Gemma's story as much as I enjoyed writing it. If you liked it, please consider leaving a review. Next up will be a novella continuing Raef and Gemma's story and their wedding. Then will come Max and Tiba's story. They have been hounding me to get their story out there. I can't wait to continue the journey with these characters.

Thanks again for reading!

— *C.*

ABOUT THE AUTHOR

Growing up in rural Louisiana, I dreamed of one day being a writer. Although it took many years to achieve that dream, life has been fulfilling along the way. Being a wife and a mother are the things I consider my biggest accomplishments. My family is number one in my eyes.

By day, I work in a public school finance. At night and on weekends, I become a writer. Outside of work and writing, I enjoy reading, photography and traveling. I am obsessed with all things Disney and Thirty Seconds to Mars. In addition to my husband and son, my three favorite men are Mickey Mouse, Jared Leto and Shannon Leto.

I can't forget to mention my two babies, Beaux—our half Yorkie, half Labrador doggie—and Kat—who is actually a cat. They complete our little family and have helped with our empty-nest since our children have become adults. They are very spoiled and have a hard time understanding why they can't be in my lap when I am writing.

CONNECT WITH C. KAYE

Email:
authorckaye@gmail.com

Website:
www.authorckaye.wixsite.com/ckaye

Facebook:
www.facebook.com/profile.
php?id=100012932410818
&
www.facebook.com/C-Kaye-281390712238288/

Twitter:
www.twitter.com/authorckaye

Instagram:
www.instagram.com/authorc.kaye/